Mi̇

Home core,
enjoy!

THE MILL POND

JUNE 2/2018

www.ronbase.com
Read Ron's blog at
www.ronbase.wordpress.com
Contact Ron at
ronbase@ronbase.com

THE MILL POND

A Novel of Suspense

Ron Base

West-End Books

Copyright © 2018 Ron Base

Library and Archives Canada Cataloguing in Publication

Base, Ron, 1948-, author

The Mill Pond / Ron Base.

Sequel to: The escarpment.
ISBN 978-0-9940645-5-4 (softcover)

I. Title.

PS8553.A784M55 2018   C813'.54   C2018-902212-4

West-End Books
133 Mill St.
Milton, Ontario
L9T 1S1

Cover design and co-ordination: Jennifer Smith
Text design and electronic formatting: Ric Base
Author photograph: Jay Buchanan

First Edition

By the pricking of my thumbs
Something wicked this way comes.

William Shakespeare, *Macbeth*

PRESENT DAY

1.

The world is full of dead bodies.

There was even a dead body at the Mill Pond, just about the last place anyone would imagine finding such a thing.

Jean Whitlock did not want to find that body.

She fervently hoped someone else would. But as she jogged along the embankment beside the pond, she found herself alone, and there was the body that could not be ignored.

Female, wedged between a rotting, waterlogged tree trunk and the shore, lichen and water lilies gently pushing against it.

Jean slowed her run, considered just keeping going, then decided against it—someone could be watching, and that would look suspicious—and fished her cellphone from her shorts. The 911 operator was on the line almost immediately. Jean stated her name and said there was a deceased female lying in the water at the edge of the Mill Pond in Milton. The nine-one-one operator asked her to stay put and said that police officers were on their way.

Jean waited by the body. She expected another jogger or a dog walker to happen along so she wasn't alone trying to explain this to the police. As someone who had recently left the RCMP under a cloud, and who had previously been tangled up in a murder that had resulted in the death of her brother, Bryce, and a far-reaching municipal scandal, another dead body was the last thing she needed. But no one appeared. It was left to her. It was always, it seemed, left to her.

A thin sun struggled through trees just beginning to show off vivid autumn colors. Through the foliage she could see an elderly man appear on the gazebo at the far end on the pond. The man lit a cigarette, leaned against the railing momentarily, taking in the tranquility, and then moved on.

In the 1800s the town had come to life around this pond and the Jasper Martin gristmill that had encouraged others to settle in the area. A relentless populace bursting out of Toronto, spilling across the landscape, filling new developments, had all but swallowed the old Milton. The pond endured, though, a reminder of what once was, a time, Jean imagined, that didn't include a lot of dead bodies.

But then the world was full of them. Even here.

Presently, on the access road below the pathway, a Halton police cruiser appeared. A good response time, Jean thought. Of course, first thing in the morning in a town like Milton, there wasn't a whole lot to keep officers busy. Well, there was now.

The two officers trundled along to where she stood, young men with shaved heads and wary expressions; not every day they got a report of a dead body. "Jesus," said one of them, the younger of the two.

The older cop, not much more than thirty, demanded: "What's up?"

"What?" Jean couldn't believe what she was hearing from this guy.

The older officer took on a belligerent expression. "You phoned 911, lady. What's the story?" He nodded in the direction of the pond. "This the floater?"

"First of all, that's not how you deal with someone who has just found a dead body," Jean said. "You don't approach that person and ask, 'what's up?'"

The older officer looked startled. The younger guy couldn't keep his eyes off the water.

"I'm a former RCMP officer," Jean continued. "So, I know something about how you should respond to a scene like this. You do it with a lot more courtesy than you two are demonstrating."

The younger cop turned away from the body, his face softening. "You're a police officer?"

"Used to be," Jean replied.

"I don't like your attitude," the older cop said, fighting to hold in his temper.

The younger cop ignored him and asked, "What time did you find the body?" He had his notebook out.

"About ten minutes ago," Jean said. "Look, it's none of my business, but from what I can see, you need to get homicide detectives and forensics people in here as soon as possible."

"Why don't you mind your own goddamn business?" snapped the older cop.

"It's all right, Pete," said the younger cop patiently. He addressed Jean: "First, let's get some more information and then we can call in the cavalry. Tell me your name and how you managed to be out here this morning."

"My name is Jean Whitlock. I live not far from here on James Street. I was jogging in the park, as I do every morning."

The younger officer asked how to spell her name and then took down her address and phone number before asking, "And that's when you came across the body? As you were running?"

"That's correct."

"And you didn't touch it?"

"No," Jean answered.

By now the older cop was staring at Jean, his eyes becoming small and black. "You're not *that* Jean Whitlock, are you?"

"Which Jean Whitlock is that?" Jean demanded.

"The one that raised such a stink after she got fired from the Mounties."

Jean addressed the younger cop. "Do you need anything else from me?"

"Yeah, I thought it was you," the older cop sneered. "Not exactly a credit to your force, are you?"

"C'mon Pete," the younger cop interjected. "This lady is only trying to help us."

"Is she?"

The younger cop focused on Jean. "Just out of curiosity, Ms. Whitlock. What makes you think we should call in homicide?"

"Just a hunch," Jean said.

When she got back to the apartment she was occupying on the second floor of the Whitlock Funeral Home, Jean went into the bathroom, stripped off her jogging clothes, and stepped under a hot shower. Her cellphone started ringing as she dried herself.

That didn't take long, she thought.

"Jean, this is Detective Glen Petrusiak," the voice on the phone stated authoritatively.

"Hello, Glen," Jean said. "How have you been?" She had dealt with Petrusiak before, a straight shooter formerly with the Toronto Police Force, a no-nonsense guy who, Jean got the impression, did not think a whole lot of her.

This was not going to do much to change his mind, Jean thought.

"I'm at the Mill Pond. I understand you found the body."

"I was jogging," Jean said.

"Could you come over here?" Petrusiak asked.

"Listen, I'm simply the civilian who happened to come across a body in the water. I don't have anything more to offer."

"Do me a favor, will you, and come back? It won't take long."

"All right, give me a few minutes," Jean said.

She put the phone down, gathering her thoughts for what was to come. She dressed in jeans and a pullover, grabbed an apple from the refrigerator, and hurried down the stairs and out the front entrance. By now it was mid-morning, unseasonably warm for the time of year. The sun felt good on her skin as she walked along James Street toward the Rotary Park and the Mill Pond.

She reached the bottom of the rusted iron steps leading to the park. The two baseball diamonds to her left were deserted, the sun glistening off the dew still clinging to the greenspace between them.

As she approached the pond, she could see the assembly of police and emergency vehicles. Yellow police tape marking off a crime scene fluttered in the breeze. Jean's stomach tightened.

She told the uniformed officers guarding the staircase to the embankment path that Glen Petrusiak wanted to see her. One of the cops spoke into the microphone clipped to his chest and a couple of minutes later Petrusiak appeared at the top of the stairs, motioning for her to come forward.

Middle-aged, with a bland cop's face arranged in the sort of noncommittal expression that gave nothing away, Petrusiak wore a dark suit with a tie adorned by red and yellow circles and squares, an unexpected splash of color.

"Thanks for coming over, Jean," Petrusiak said.

"It's been a while," Jean said.

"We seem to keep meeting over dead bodies," Petrusiak said.

"Like I told you on the phone, I came across this person while I was out for a run. At about six-thirty. I then called 911. Your officers got here ten minutes later."

"Dobbs said you gave them shit," Mickey said.

"Dobbs was the younger guy?"

"That's right."

"A good cop," Jean said. "I'm not so sure about the other one."

"Come and take a look for me, will you?"

"At the body? I don't think there's much I can add to what I've already told you."

"Just have a look."

He stepped aside so that she could go up to where a dozen officers and forensic technicians in their white suits milled about. They parted as Jean approached so that she could enter the tent set up to contain the body. Petrusiak said to one of the techs, "Open it up, will you, Jimmy?"

The tech opened an end flap so that Jean could see the body lying on its back. The clothes the woman wore were still wet and streaked with dirt: black slacks, a black, long-sleeved pullover, sneakers. A deep, ugly gash around the neck area had caused a great deal of bleeding so that blood mixed with dirt saturated the pullover.

Petrusiak said, "You recognize the deceased." It was not a question.

Jean straightened, not saying anything.

Petrusiak said, "Jean. Answer me, please. Do you recognize this person or not?"

"Yes," Jean said. "Yes, I do."

"Do you have any idea how she got here?"

Jean did not answer.

THE PAST
Several Weeks Before

2

Saturday mornings, Milton's Main Street from the landmark brick pile of St. Paul's United Church east as far as Martin Street, was closed to traffic for the Farmer's Market. Part weekly gathering where neighbors met to trade local news and gossip, admire each other's dogs and children of which there were seemingly endless numbers in what remained Canada's fastest-growing town, the market was also a reminder, albeit a fading one, of Milton's farming roots.

Now with autumn coloring the distant escarpment, county farmers, beneath canopies lining either side of the street, hawked the best of the harvest. In addition to fruits and vegetables, visitors were offered artisanal honey, hand-crafted bird houses, gourmet cupcakes. They were invited to sign up for the annual Milton Film Festival, line up for a peameal bacon sandwich and support the local historical society.

As long as business was all done by noon. That's when a local councilman in a yellow vest ensured the market closed down. Naturally, the closing occurred at the moment when vendors were busiest. Fifteen minutes before twelve, Jean Whitlock could barely make her way through the young families who otherwise never strayed far from the townhouses in the new developments ringing the town, and the loyal baby boomers who formed the town's backbone and kept events such as the market alive.

Earlier, Jean had indulged herself with a wash and a cut nearby at the Studio, Omid working his magic, leaving her curiously refreshed and renewed, ready to take on the world. Loaded down with vine-ripened tomatoes, a cabbage, a dozen McIntosh apples, her final stop would be the husband-and-wife beekeepers across the street from Village Bikes and Skis where she had recently bought the custom-built Surly bike she swore she was going to ride—soon.

She was headed there when she saw him.

Royal Canadian Mounted Police Sergeant Adam Machota, wearing a dark pea coat, smiled as he started toward her.

She stopped dead, a cold fear running along her spine. "Jean," Machota said. "I thought it was you. Isn't this market something? It's my first time here. So glad I've discovered it. How are you doing?"

"Get out of here," she managed.

"I hope you're all right," Machota continued. "I heard you've had some trouble."

"Do you hear me, Machota? I want you to stay away from me."

Machota's grin grew wider. He was a handsome, dark-haired man in his mid-thirties but that smile, despite its best intentions, gave him an air of nastiness; not misplaced in Jean's estimation.

"I was sorry to hear about the death of your brother," he went on. "I understand that your mother is also deceased. It never rains but it pours, I guess."

"You bastard," Jean said. "I want you to leave me alone."

"I'm going to be in town for a while, Jean," Machota went on. "If there's anything I can do for you, please let me know."

Jean tried to go past him. The surrounding crowd pressed in, demanding kids, baby carriages, eager dogs tugging at the end of leashes. Machota shifted so that he was in her way. "I know this is a trying time for you, Jean. What with your emotional problems, it can't be easy. I want you to think of me as a shoulder you can lean on. I'm here to tell you I'm a friend, not an enemy."

"Get out of my way."

"I can be your friend, Jean, or I can be something else. You decide which. If I'm your friend and we agree that nothing has to be said beyond that, all your troubles go away. But if for some reason, you decide to think of me as an adversary, well, I'm sure you don't want that."

"Fuck off," Jean said.

"It's great to see you," Machota said, his smile brightening even more. "You are really looking good. Think about what I said. I'll be in touch."

He turned and melted into the surrounding throng. Seething, Jean took a deep breath, suddenly feeling very much alone on a crowded street in the town where she was born and grew up.

―――――

Jean could not remember a time when she didn't dream of becoming a Mountie. She had grown up in Milton, the daughter of Ida and Eric Whitlock. The Whitlock family had been in the funeral business for generations. Unlike her brother, Bryce, Jean early on had decided the family business was not for her, even though, to please her father, she had trained to be a funeral director.

But her true ambition was the RCMP. She had been a good officer, too, impressing everyone she worked with. Her performance had led to the Afghanistan assignment, aiding and training the Afghan National Police (ANP). The job was frustrating but by the end of her six-month stint in Kandahar, she felt as though some progress had been made, particularly her work with Major Shaar Zorn, a tough, charismatic police veteran.

On Jean's last night in Kandahar, she had dined with her superior, Sergeant Adam Machota, who had overseen her performance for the past six months. They had stuffed themselves with lamb and *bulani*— fried bread pockets filled with vegetables. Machota said that Major Zorn had invited them to his home in an upscale neighborhood of the city for a farewell drink. They had driven to the house together.

When they got to the house, Major Zorn was not home. They no sooner had entered than Sergeant Machota had grabbed her, smashed her against the wall, tore at her clothes, threw her to the floor and tried to rape her.

Jean had managed to knock Machota unconscious using her police baton moments before masked gunmen invaded the house. Trading gunfire with the intruders, she managed to get the semi-conscious Machota out of the house and into their vehicle and escape.

They were driving through the streets of Kandahar when the sergeant, having regained consciousness, shot her and left her for dead.

It was Major Shaar Zorn who had saved her life after finding her lying in the street, badly wounded and rushing her to a nearby hospital. She should have been a hero. Sergeant Machota should have gone to prison. Instead, the Force chose to cover up the incident. Jean was forced out. Sergeant Machota was allowed to remain a Mountie.

When she decided to go to the media with her story, she became a sensation for a few weeks. And then the story had more or less died in the face of the smear campaign mounted against her by the Force.

A thorough internal investigation had failed to substantiate Corporal Whitlock's story, the Force maintained. The Afghan police major she claimed could testify on her behalf had disappeared. Sergeant Machota claimed that he had saved Jean's life that night, fighting off the gunmen who had shot her.

She had eventually convinced herself that the unfairness of it all no longer rankled. That she had moved on. She would never have to see Sergeant Machota again. She could get on with her life.

Until now.

Now Machota had come to Milton.

3

Back home, in the small house behind the funeral home she had moved into following her brother's death, Jean made herself coffee, trying to shake off the nightmare image of Adam Machota. Except this was no nightmare. This was a real and present danger, a man who had already attempted to rape her and then tried to kill her.

That bastard she thought, sitting at the kitchen table with the coffee, how dare he invade her life again. Why would he come here to Milton? To scare her obviously, trying once again to shut her up. Only she wasn't going to shut up.

Perhaps Machota had decided that if she would not be quiet, he would ...what? What was he planning? He was crazy enough to do just about anything.

The question was, what could *she* do? She set her coffee aside, deep in thought. Not that it was going to do much good, but she should at least make the phone call. Let them know what was happening.

She found the Ottawa number in one of the notebooks she had kept during the inquiry into events in Kandahar that had led to her ouster from the Force. She took a deep breath and then made the call she thought she would never make again.

To her surprise, Inspector Jill Lowry came on the line almost immediately, crisply announcing her name.

She had been the woman grilling her during the inquiry, the grandmother type with the blessing smile who at least gave an impression of sympathy, unlike her male counterparts. But Jean had suspected that was her role, the good Mountie, one woman bonding with another.

Her real job, it became apparent, had been to shut down the controversy as quickly as possible, ushering Jean Whitlock off the media stage and out of the Force. Lowry had accomplished this with consummate skill. Still, if Jean was going to receive a hearing from anyone on the Force, Inspector Jill Lowry was her best bet.

"Inspector Lowry, it's Jean Whitlock calling." Jean had to stop herself from identifying by rank: *Corporal* Jean Whitlock.

Inspector Lowy allowed a lengthy pause before she said, "Yes, Jean."

"Have you got a moment to talk?"

"Yes, of course. How can I help you?" Crisp. Professional. Neutral. Vintage Inspector Lowry.

"I'm in Milton," Jean said.

"Yes, so I understand. The town where you grew up. How are you doing there?"

"Not very well," Jean said. "That's why I'm calling. I'm in Milton but so is Adam Machota."

That produced silence on the other end of the line.

Jean said, "Inspector? Are you there?"

"Yes, I'm right here, Jean. When did you see Sergeant Machota?"

"An hour ago. He confronted me on the street and made threats."

"Threats? What kind of threats?"

"Nothing specific. He wants to be my friend. But if I'm not going to be his friend then he's going to be my enemy. That sort of thing."

"There was no specific threat?"

"The fact that he's here, talking to me, is itself a threat. He's not supposed to come near me, and yet here he is."

"Yes, I understand what you're saying." There was a note of sympathy in Inspector Lowry's voice. "As far as I know, Sergeant Machota has been stationed in Ottawa. I don't know what he would be doing in Milton."

"I know what he's doing, Inspector. He's here to threaten me into keeping quiet."

"He shouldn't be there and he certainly shouldn't be talking to you," Inspector Lowry said. "It's the weekend but let me see if I can get some answers. Can I reach you at this number?"

"Yes."

"How are you doing otherwise, Jean?" The sympathy level in her voice had raised somewhat. "I understand there's been some disruption in your life."

Yes, Jean thought. You might say that. The death of her brother. Mother gone. Seemingly endless turbulence that, with the appearance of Adam Machota, didn't look as though it would soon end.

"There's been a lot of turmoil," Jean said aloud. "But I'm getting through."

"Are you taking on some sort of private investigative role in Milton?" Inspector Lowry asked.

"Nothing like that," Jean said. "Like I told you, just trying to get through. Nothing more."

"All right, Jean. Let me get back to you."

4

Adam Machota dropped his suitcase and briefcase to the floor and surveyed the Best Western hotel room he and Reagan had just checked into. She placed her bag on the king-size bed, making a face as she took in the room with its view of the parking lot. "What a dump," she said.

"Bette Davis," Machota said.

"Huh?"

"Bette Davis. It's a line she supposedly used in the movies, although I don't think she actually did."

"Never heard of her," Reagan said.

With her soft, round face framed by shiny dark brown hair and that body poured into tight jeans and a loose tank top, Machota should have been a lot more excited. But then she would say something like "never heard of her," and the excitement drained right out of him, replaced by agitation.

He thought of Jean Whitlock. The short noontime encounter with her had excited him more than anything. Jean would never agitate him, he was certain of that. She might hate him, but she would never stick in his craw the way Reagan Elliott tended to do.

But Reagan had her place here, and she was agreeable to that, so for now he would put up with her and her lack of worldly knowledge. After all, if she were any smarter, she probably wouldn't have agreed to play along.

"How long are we going to be here?" She slid over to him, hand on his chest. He was assailed by the cloying scent of her.

"As long as it takes," he said.

"You're too rough with me." She kissed his neck. He thought of Jean.

"What you like," he said.

"Sometimes." Her hand was on his crotch. Jean, he thought. Jean.

There was a rap on the door. Machota heaved a silent sigh of relief.

"That's Moose," Machota said.

Reagan's hand moved away. She made a frown. "I don't like that guy. He scares me."

"That's the idea behind Moose."

Machota opened the door to admit Richard "Moose" Haggerty, former Montreal biker arriving in a fog of stale cigarette smoke. Moose Haggerty had a brush cut and a weathered, smoker's face. He wore a gold earring in his right earlobe, a silver skull ring on his left index finger, and if he weren't currently dressed in a long-sleeved black shirt, you could inspect the cobra tattoos up and down his arms. Might be a good idea to tone him down a bit before sending him onto the streets of Milton, Machota thought. Or maybe he'd fit right in.

"All checked in?" Machota asked.

"This the best you can do, chief?" Moose demanded in that gravelly voice cured by thousands of cigarettes. "Did you know you can't smoke in this hotel?"

Machota shook his head. "What's wrong with the two of you? You'd think you're used to staying at the Ritz the way you're carrying on."

"What's the Ritz?" Reagan wanted to know.

"What's the story here, chief?" Moose addressed Machota. "What are we doing?"

Machota lifted his briefcase onto a table by the window and removed a file folder. He laid it on the table and flipped it open. There was a photograph of Jean Whitlock in her Mountie uniform.

"This is the woman I was telling you about," Machota said, tapping the photo.

"She's one of your asshole Mounties?" Moose was shaking his head.

"*Former* Mountie. We worked together in Afghanistan."

"She's cute," pronounced Reagan. "Even in that stupid uniform."

"I love her," Machota said.

Reagan looked at him in astonishment. "You *love* her?"

"I admire her," Machota said. "She's highly intelligent, disciplined, everything you would look for in an officer and a woman."

Reagan was not to be deterred. "But you love her?"

"Like I explained earlier, Jean Whitlock is the subject of an undercover investigation," Machota said.

"I'm leading that investigation. The two of you are going to assist me in carrying it out."

"Jeez," Reagan said. "How do you treat the women you don't love?"

Machota kept his eyes on the file folder. "That's what we're doing here," he said.

Moose said, "What the hell do you need us for?"

Machota took his eyes off the file and looked impatient. "I told you, we're working off the grid, and that could entail activities that would fall outside the purview of the usual police investigation."

"In other words, you've got us to do any dirty work that needs doing," Moose said.

"You're here because the two of you don't want to go to jail," Machota snapped. "You're here to do as I tell you, and not ask too many questions."

"I don't like it when I can't ask questions," Moose said. "That's the kind of miserable bastard I am." He was facing Machota, not blinking his eyes.

Reagan noticed Adam didn't seem at all intimidated by Moose. He produced a lazy smile. "You're not going to give me trouble, are you Moose?"

"Not me. I'm no trouble at all."

"Glad to hear it," Machota said. "That way, we'll get this done and the two of you will be free to get on with your lives."

"I like that," Reagan interjected brightly.

Machota focused on Moose. "What about you, Moose? Do you like that?'

Moose forced a smile. "Sure," he said.

5

Jean's phone started to vibrate. She thought it might be Inspector Jill Lowry calling back and swiped it open, immediately regretting she did.

"Jean, hello, this is Grace Travis over at the mayor's office," said the voice on the phone. Grace Travis had worked for her uncle since Jean was a teenager; the trusted keeper of the mayor's agenda, and, Jean suspected, of his secrets. If anyone knew where the bodies were buried around Milton, it was Grace Travis.

"Grace," Jean said.

"It's been a while since we've talked," Grace said in that familiar, cheerful voice that never failed to sound sincere, even though she was working for a man who almost never was sincere, no matter how he sounded.

"Yes, it has," said Jean in as non-committal a voice as she could summon.

"The mayor would like to see you," Grace went on. "Are you available this afternoon?"

She wanted to say no, she was not available any longer to Mayor Jock Whitlock. She was unavailable to the man who had lied to her, who had tried to protect Del Caulder, the wealthy local developer now imprisoned having been found guilty of sex crimes and fraud. Jock Whitlock was someone she wanted to stay as far away from as she could.

At least that's what she told herself.

Except it was the siren call of her uncle; a call she had been unable to resist all her life, and so, despite herself, she said, "Yes."

"He'll meet you at the usual place," Grace said brightly. "About four o'clock?"

Jean hesitated, more for effect than anything else; a lame attempt to show Grace she was her own person, that she didn't come running just because her uncle snapped his fingers.

When she felt she had paused long enough, Jean said, "Yes, that's fine."

The usual place recently had been renovated. New paving stones had been set to form a handsome promenade past the old City Hall. The gazebo had been spruced up, too, flowers planted and the park benches replaced with newer, more comfortable models.

Mayor Jock wasn't on his usual bench this time. He was seated further back off one of the pathways winding through the flower gardens. It was more private back here, Jean surmised. Jock was less likely to encounter citizens unhappy with a controversial mayor, his image tarnished by recent events.

Jock might be suffering for his crimes, Jean thought as she approached. He'd put on weight and his complexion was as gray as the afternoon sky full of autumn threat. Even his clothes didn't seem to quite fit. His belly bulged over his belt, straining the striped dress shirt. His suit jacket looked too small as he hunched forward on the bench, a paper bag in his lap.

He rallied a smile when Jean sat down beside him. "I was beginning to think you wouldn't show up," he said.

"I almost didn't," Jean replied.

"But here you are," Jock said.

"Here I am."

"I didn't bring you a tuna sandwich," Jock said. "You may wonder why I didn't bring you a tuna sandwich."

"I really don't care, Jock."

He ignored her. "I didn't bring you a tuna sandwich because the last time, you didn't eat it. You threw it away. The waste of a good sandwich."

"It's late in the afternoon, Jock. What is it you want?"

"You don't eat sandwiches in the afternoon?" He seemed mildly amused by her statement.

He opened the paper bag on his lap. "I brought you a donut." He held it up as though presenting evidence. "Homemade. One of the women in the office."

"I don't want a donut, Jock."

He shrugged and took a bite. "Not bad," he decided before stealing a glance at her. "You're still angry, I can see that."

"Do me a favor, will you? Don't tell me what I am or am not."

He nodded and took another mouthful of donut before dropping it into the bag. "Actually, they're not that good. I can do better at Tim Horton's."

He rose from the bench, hobbling over to a municipal garbage can to deposit the bag into it. "Don't tell,

Grace," he said, resuming his seat. "She wants me to lose some weight."

The short walk had left him winded; much of the vitality Jean had grown up admiring seemed to have drained out of him. He was the ghost of Jock Whitlock.

"Are you all right?" Jean asked, worried despite herself.

"Arthritis is acting up again, and they keep telling me I should never have played high school football because I need knee and hip surgery sooner than later, but otherwise I'm fine."

"You should get that looked at."

"Everyone tells me the same thing. Good advice and one of these days I'm going to listen to it. What about you?"

"I'm fine."

"You sure about that?"

"I hear you may lose the election."

Jock seemed slightly taken back. "Me? Perish the thought." He grinned and then added: "Well, it's been a long run, so what the hell. We'll see."

"What's the trouble, Jock? Why am I sitting here beside you watching you throw away donuts?"

He shifted on the bench as though her question had made him uncomfortable. "This is embarrassing," he said.

"I would have thought you're beyond embarrassment at this point," Jean said.

"Not quite, I'm afraid."

"No?"

"My wife's having an affair." The words came out in a rush so that Jean nearly didn't catch them. When they did register, she wasn't sure what to say.

"Did you hear me?" he asked.

"Desiree, the much younger wife. Desiree who everyone warned you not to marry."

"Try not to rub it in," Jock said grimly.

"I'm sorry, I shouldn't have said that. Are you sure about this?"

"Not entirely, no. That's why I called you."

"You didn't call me, Jock. Your secretary did. I don't know how I can help with your marital problems."

"You've got a law enforcement background. You were a very good cop—*are* a very good cop. You're also discreet, one of the family. I can trust you, and that's something I can't say about anyone else in this town."

"I don't understand what trusting me has to do with anything," Jean said.

"I'd like you to follow her," Jock said. "Find out who she's seeing."

Jean gave him a hard look. "Are you crazy? I'm not going to do something like that."

"I know I'm asking a lot. You don't owe me a thing. I understand that. But I'm still your uncle and I need your help."

"Following your wife around isn't helping you, Jock."

"Then tell me what I should do. This is driving me crazy."

"I'm no expert on relationships," Jean said. "But why don't you try asking her?"

"Because I'm afraid that will just make things worse." He swung his heavy body to her, his face haggard and imploring. She had never seen him like this. The absence of the confident, aggressive Uncle Jock unnerved her.

"Please," Jock said. "Please do this for me."

"This is not what I want to be doing," she said.

"It's not what I want you doing, either, believe me. But I have to know. If I know, if I've got the facts in front of me, then I'll have an understanding of what I have to do."

"Let me think about it," she said.

Jock's face fell. "That's another way of saying no."

"It's my way of deciding if I want to do this."

"She goes to the GoodLife Fitness gym on Steeles every Monday, Wednesday and Friday. If something's happening, that could be where it started."

"If I do this Jock, if I start to poke around, what am I going to find out about you?"

"Me?" This time he looked genuinely surprised. "Why would any of this have to do with me?"

"This didn't happen in a vacuum. Happy women don't have affairs. Unhappy women have them."

"You have a lot of experience with this sort of thing, do you?"

Jean got to her feet. "I'll tell you what my experience is, Jock. My experience is that once you start to look into one thing, you end up discovering a lot of other things."

"I'm willing to take that risk."

"Are you?"

"Will you help me, Jean?"

"Like I said, I'll think about it."

"I appreciate anything you can do," Jock said.

He rose to embrace her. She jerked away from him. "Don't touch me," she said. "Don't ever touch me."

6

The Milton Evergreen Cemetery had been part of the town practically since its incorporation in the late 1600s. The Whitlock family had always buried their friends and neighbors here and then buried themselves.

Jean's mother Ida was interred beside her husband, Eric, and son, Bryce. Jean laid flowers at each of the headstones, although, if they were watching, Jean suspected only her mother would truly appreciate the gesture—the daisies being her favorite flower.

Jean was never quite sure what to do after she had placed the flowers. Kneel and pray? Pray to what? For what? Life everlasting?

Ha!

A visit to these graves should have provided the time for the meditation and reflection the funeral brochures advertised. She stood trying to meditate and reflect, to summon images and memories. Well, not too many memories. Lingering over Whitlock family history inevitably led to a dark place she would rather avoid. She didn't want to think about Bryce, for example; too painful. She didn't want to think about her own life either.

Even more painful.

She was alone; no career, no man, no real life, no prospects. And now, no family. Not that she had exactly embraced close family ties. One of the reasons she had joined the Mounties was to escape what she considered the stifling conservatism of the small town where she had grown up. She had left her family, and now her family had left her. A sense of aloneness swept over her.

So much for meditation and reflection.

There was still Uncle Jock and his two grown children, she supposed. But she wasn't so sure he counted any more, not in her life, anyway.

Jean thought about him, his hangdog look, his desperation over Desiree. Could she be having an affair? Of course, she could—and most likely was. It wasn't Jean's business. She had enough problems, even if you didn't include Adam Machota.

But then she had no choice but to include him.

A few minutes later, steering her late brother's van north on Martin Street, she reached Steele's Avenue and turned east, towards the GoodLife Fitness Centre. Before she could tell herself not to, she turned onto the roadway and parked near the entrance. It was Wednesday afternoon, one of the days Jock had said Desiree visited the gym.

The parking lot was full. Jean reached the end and was turning around when she saw an Audi sedan pull out of a parking space.

Desiree Whitlock was behind the wheel.

Okay, Jean thought, here was the wife in question directly in front of her. Jean wasn't tailing her west on Steeles Avenue, merely happening to be behind her.

When Desiree reached Martin Street, she turned south and drove to Mill and made a right turn. She went along to James, swung left and then, to Jean's amazement, turned into the funeral home and parked. Jean pulled up beside the Audi as Desiree stepped out.

Resplendent in lululemon yoga pants and hoodie, Desiree's blond hair was pulled back in a neat pony tail that made her look more like a cheerleader than an unfaithful wife.

Jean got out of the van, plastering on a smile as Desiree approached, a cellphone pressed to her ear. "No, it's simple, Marcia. Just look under the doormat at the back. The key is there. Yes. It's where I left it for you."

Desiree closed down her cellphone. "The cleaning lady," she announced "Couldn't find the housekey for this shitty house we have to live in until the new place is built.

"I'm all sweaty," she added, before she embraced Jean.

"This is a surprise," Jean said.

Desiree pulled away. Her face was grim. "Are you busy?"

"No," Jean said. "I was at the cemetery. You want to come in and have a coffee?"

"I'd like a drink," Desiree pronounced.

"I've got some wine."

"Perfect."

"Is everything all right?"

Tears sprang into Desiree's eyes. "No," she said. "Everything is shit."

7

They settled into the comfortable living room, Bryce's room, full of Bryce memories; not Jean's space at all. There was nothing of her in this house. Plenty of Bryce, a little of her parents, but she was a ghost in the shell of what was left of the family.

Jean shook off those thoughts and concentrated on Desiree, the perfection of that tear-stained face, wondering all over again what had ever attracted her to Jock. Money? He had some money, enough to build a fine new house below the escarpment. But sufficient to keep someone like Desiree in the lifestyle she almost certainly demanded? There had been rumors for years about Jock's hands in many different tills, particularly in the ones owned by the developer Del Caulder, now an inmate at Maplehurst Correction Complex, or, as it was more popularly known, the Milton Hilton.

Power? Well, the power of a local mayor; the power to attend every ribbon cutting and official opening imaginable; the power to sit through interminable council meetings debating zoning regulations; not the kind of power a woman like Desiree likely understood. So, what was it?

Jean had no answer and Desiree had been impossible to read on the matter; not an easy young woman to even like, as far as Jean was concerned. She tried to think of what would surprise her more than Desiree turning up in tears. Perhaps Desiree's husband asking his niece to find out if his wife was having an affair.

Yes, that would do the trick.

Desiree held the glass of red wine Jean had poured for her. The wine served its purpose and somewhat stifled the tears. She gulped a goodly amount before she said, "I know you don't think much of me, Jean, and I guess I haven't been the biggest fan of yours, either."

In the face of that kind of truth, Jean didn't know what to say, and so she said nothing, waiting for Desiree.

"But the thing is, I know what you've been through lately, and how unfair it is, and we're both women outnumbered in a world of men, right? And we should stick together, don't you think?"

"I wouldn't have thought you had too much difficulty operating in a man's world," Jean said dryly.

Desiree's eyes welled again, making Jean immediately sorry for what she said.

"You see that's where you're wrong," Desiree burbled. "Other women look at me and they think certain things, you know, that everything is so easy, and it isn't. Lately, things have been very difficult."

More tears. Followed by sniffles. Followed by loud gulps. "Shit," Desiree said. "I swore I wasn't going to do this. You don't have a tissue, do you?"

Jean got up and went into the kitchen. She was back a moment later with a box of Kleenex. Desiree blew her nose loudly and then used more tissues to wipe at the tears on her face. She gulped a couple of more times, sipped some wine, and then trained watery eyes on Jean. "Sorry," she said.

"Tell me what's wrong, Desiree."

"It's this…" and her voice trailed off into a succession of hiccups and more nose blowing.

"What is it?" Jean asked.

"There are these people," Desiree continued. "They say they have things…"

"What kind of things?"

"You know I've been having a lot of trouble with Jock ever since your brother died, and Del Caulder went to jail, and we were accused of all sorts of things that just weren't true."

She paused to see if any of that elicited a response from Jean. It didn't.

"So now there are more things. Things against me."

"Are they true?"

"Let's put it this way, I don't want to take the chance that they are."

"What do they want?"

"What else?" Desiree answered. "Money, of course."

"How much?

"Twenty-five thousand as a down payment. They said they would show me what they have and then we'd go from there."

"What would make someone believe you can be blackmailed?"

The question produced more tears, more tissues, still more nose blowing.

"Desiree, come on," Jean said impatiently. "You don't have to do this."

That settled her somewhat, enough to say, "I've done things I shouldn't have, I guess. But Jock's been such a bastard, and I was feeling so bad. So, shit, yeah, I've been a bad girl on occasion."

"How bad?"

"Bad enough that I don't want Jock to find out if I can help it."

"Do you have twenty-five thousand dollars?"

"That's not a problem," Desiree said, amid more sniffling.

At that point, Jean nearly told Desiree that Jock was already suspicious his wife was having an affair, but quickly decided not to say anything. Such a revelation, in her estimation, would only complicate matters that were already too complicated.

"I'm not sure how I can help," Jean said, echoing the argument she had given Jock without much success.

"Believe me, you can," Desiree insisted.

"Tell me," Jean countered.

"I'm supposed to bring the money tomorrow night. I don't want to do it alone. You're a former police officer. You're used to dealing with things like this."

Jean wasn't but didn't say anything. Instead, she asked, "Where are you supposed to meet?"

"A church parking lot in Acton, just north of here."

"What time is this supposed to happen?"

"Eight o'clock." Desiree's face filled with expectation, and something else—hope. "Please, Jean, come with me. I'm scared."

"Of who? Who is behind this?"

Desiree shook her head. "Right now, I'm not sure. I don't know whether it's real or a joke or what. If you're there, you can help me make sense of it."

"I'm not sure you should even go under these circumstances," Jean said.

"I don't feel like I've got a choice. But at least I'll be a lot safer with you there. You've got one of those baton things, right? Jock says you know how to handle yourself in a dangerous situation."

"I'm not so sure about that," Jean said.

"That's what Jock told me," Desiree said insistently.

"You know, the easiest way to deal with this, and avoid having to pay blackmail money, is to tell Jock."

Desiree shook her head vehemently. "Jock's crazy these days. He'd kill me, and once he's done that, he'll divorce me."

"He loves you," Jean said.

"It's not the right kind of love," Desiree said. "It's the kind of love where if I do as I'm told, he's fine. But as soon as I stand up for myself or do something he doesn't like, he's a crazy man."

"Here's what I'll do," Jean said. "I'll be in Acton tonight."

Desiree's face flooded with relief.

"But after that, you agree to talk to Jock. I'll go with you and be there when you tell him what's happened."

"I don't know," Desiree said morosely. "You may think you know Jock, but you don't know him the way I do. There's all sorts of strange shit going down right now. I'm not sure where he's at with any of it."

"Let's find out," Jean said.

"I don't want to divorce him," Desiree said. "I don't want that."

"I don't think Jock wants that, either."

"You'll be there tomorrow night?"

"If you agree to talk to Jock."

Desiree smiled brightly through her tears and then threw her arms around Jean, hugging her tightly.

"You really are my friend," Desiree burbled. "You truly are."

In a million years, Jean never would have expected to hear *that* from Desiree.

8

Inspector Jill Lowry phoned Jean the next morning. The previous sympathy in her voice had been replaced by formality. "Sergeant Machota is on leave from the Force," she announced.

"What does that mean?" Jean demanded.

"The sergeant requested a leave, and it's been granted, so we don't know where he is or what his plans are."

"He's here in Milton and his plans are to harass and threaten me," Jean said.

Inspector Lowry's voice retained its neutral distance. "But from what you told me previously, Sergeant Machota has made no specific threat. Is that correct?"

"Not in so many words. He's not stupid. He hasn't come right out and said anything. But his presence in town implies a threat."

"Unfortunately, there is nothing we can act on," Inspector Lowry said.

"Inspector Lowry, this man first tried to rape me and then he shot me. You know and I know he shouldn't be anywhere near me and yet here he is."

The inspector's voice retained its icy neutrality. "As I told you, the sergeant is on leave, and he can go wherever he wants. As long as he doesn't break any laws we have no right to dictate his movements."

"Thank you, inspector," Jean said coldly. And hung up.

She should have known they wouldn't do anything. If they cared about her, she would still be a member of the Force. She was on her own; from the moment Machota attacked her inside that Kandahar house she basically had been alone, except for Major Shaar Zorn, the Afghan police officer who had saved her life. But he was far away. It was up to her, she decided. She would survive by relying on herself.

Upstairs in her bedroom closet, Jean removed a cardboard box from the top shelf. She set the box on the bed, lifted the lid to remove a Ruger .45 semi-automatic pistol and an expandable police baton. She held the gun in her hand, made sure it was loaded, and then took the baton and the .45 down to the kitchen.

The .45 went into a drawer where it was readily accessible. She placed the baton on the counter, against the backsplash.

Ensuring weapons were available in case of trouble made her feel better. But she had to be careful. The Force had taken the position that she was a renegade who caused trouble. Part of that perception had been fueled by the media; nonetheless, any action she took to protect herself could get her into a whole lot more trouble.

She thought for a while, deciding there was one more person who might help her. She picked up her cellphone. Mickey Dann answered almost immediately. "This is a surprise," he said.

"How are you?"

"Like I said. Surprised."

"What? You never expected to hear from me again?"

"Yeah, something like that."

"Is there any chance we could get together?"

"Don't tell me you're asking me on a date."

"It's not a date-date," Jean said. "It's an I-need-to-talk-to-you lunch. I'm buying."

"You're not trying to bribe a police officer, are you?"

Mickey's attempt to turn this into a flirtatious encounter annoyed her. "I do need to talk to you," she said.

"Okay," he said soberly. "Where and when?"

They decided on Pasqualino's, the Italian restaurant on Main Street. Mickey was waiting for her. A few minutes after one p.m., the restaurant was only half full, the canned music kept low so that conversation was possible. One of Pasqualino's many attractions, in addition to the dependably fine food, Jean thought, as she sat down, was the absence of giant LCD screens featuring intense young men careening around hockey rinks, soccer and football fields.

"You're looking good," Mickey said appreciatively as she formally shook his hand, deciding what it was about him she found kind of attractive. *Sort* of attractive. A hint of Steve McQueen cool? A trace of Bruce Willis tough guy? There was the slightly world-weary expression of a cop in his forties, dressed in the shabby-chic uniform of your average detective: the brown suit that had fit when Mickey bought it; now, not so much. A nondescript tie that had seen better days; white shirt, frayed at the collar. Someone needed to take Mickey Dann shopping, she decided.

A server presented them with menus and asked if they'd like something to drink.

Mickey raised his eyebrows in her direction. "What about a glass of wine?"

"Are you having something?"

"I'm on the job, but you go ahead."

"It's all right," Jean said to the server. "Just some sparkling water, please."

"Tap water for me," Mickey said. He looked at Jean. "Are you ready to order?"

Burrata with olive oil and cherry tomato salsa with croutons for her; a wood-fired pizza for law enforcement. The server left, reducing them to awkward silence.

"How've you been?" As good an ice-breaker as anything, Jean guessed.

"Things have finally quietened down," Mickey replied. "After being convinced I would probably lose my job, it looks as though they're going to let me hang on, although the department brass certainly has their eyes on me."

"You did put the region's biggest developer in jail and he's probably going away for a long time. That should make you some sort of hero, shouldn't it?"

Mickey gave a snort of laughter. "I'm not sure what it makes me, but it certainly doesn't make me any kind of hero. If it were up to my bosses, I'd be gone. But I'm still standing, so, to hell with them."

"I know the feeling," Jean said.

"What about you? How are you doing?"

"Getting through, I suppose. Dealing with a whole lot of things, the sale of the funeral home, my brother's death, my mother's. Accountants. Lawyers. A lot of mundane stuff, but it keeps me busy."

The server was back with the water, promising their meals would be out in a few minutes.

"There's something else," Jean said as Mickey drank his water.

"Okay," he said, setting his glass to one side.

"Another problem, this one more serious."

"So, my irresistible charm isn't the reason I'm having lunch with you," Mickey said, giving her a smile that took some of the world weariness out of his face.

"Nothing to do with your charm," she said.

"No? Then what is it?"

"Adam Machota," she answered.

9

Reagan parked her rental car on Charles Street and then walked around the corner to the restaurant. She peered in the big picture window and saw that Jean was inside with a male, his back to her. She called Machota.

"She's in a restaurant with some guy," Reagan said.

"How long have they been there?" Machota asked.

"I dunno, not long, I guess. There's no food on the table or anything. What do you want me to do?"

"Stay put. Phone me as soon as they leave."

"For your information, I don't think she's all that cute."

"She's not cute," Machota said. "She's beautiful."

"I don't want to hang around here," Reagan said petulantly.

"Do as you're told," Machota snapped and then hung up.

"Shit," Reagan said.

The server brought their food. Jean poked at the burrata but otherwise didn't touch it. She noticed Mickey was no longer smiling. "What about Machota?" he asked.

"He's in town. He's been in touch with me."

"This is your sergeant in Afghanistan, the guy who tried to rape you."

"Not to forget the part where he shot me," Jean added.

"Yeah, we shouldn't forget that part," Mickey agreed. "Have you been in touch with the Mounties?"

She nodded. "But they're not going to do anything."

"You're kidding. Why not?"

"He's on a leave of absence," Jean said. "They say there's nothing they can do."

Mickey used a knife and fork to cut into his pizza.

Jean couldn't help but smile. "I didn't realize you were so refined, Mickey."

"Hey, I'm in a good restaurant with an attractive woman. I'm on my best behavior." He used the fork to shove some pizza in his mouth. He chewed it and then put his fork aside. "This Machota, he's a professional, an experienced police officer, right?"

"Correct," Jean said. "The Force certainly values him a whole lot more than me."

"Then I don't understand why he would put his job on the line to come after you."

"I don't get it either," Jean admitted. "I could never understand why he acted the way he did in Kandahar. The attack came out of nowhere. One moment, I was with a fellow officer, sharing food with him after completing a tough assignment. The next, that same officer transformed into this monster tearing at my clothes, trying to rape me. No warning, no explanation, no nothing."

"It doesn't make a lot of sense, but then rape never does," Mickey said.

"Having gotten away with trying to rape and then murder me, he isn't satisfied. Apparently, he wants more."

"More of what?"

"More of me," Jean said.

"Shit," Mickey said. "This isn't good."

"No, it's not."

"Maybe there's something I can do," Mickey said.

"What? Arrest him for being in Milton?"

"No, but I can at least talk to him. Let him know that police are aware of his presence and are keeping an eye on his activities."

"I'm not sure that's going to do much good."

"He's a working police officer so he's got to be careful, even if he is off-duty." Mickey shrugged. "It's worth a try—better than you shooting him."

"I'm not going to shoot him, but let's wait and see what he does," Jean said.

"But you don't think he'll leave you alone."

"No, I don't."

"Then I should talk to him."

"Let him make the first move. See what he does."

"Supposing his first move is making you dead?"

"Then you'll know who to arrest," Jean replied.

10

Machota inserted the pick, bent at the end, into the middle of the lock and then slowly withdrew it until he heard a clicking sound. He shoved a tension wrench into the bottom of the lock, at the same time moving the pick back into place, turning the wrench until the deadbolt slid back enabling him to open the door.

He was surprised. He thought Jean would have installed a more formidable lock to protect her house. One of those Israeli deals featuring floating or magnetic tumblers with carbide plates that can't be penetrated by a drill. But in spite of her police training, Jean was, like most people, careless.

Not him. Not Adam Machota. Adam Machota was not careless.

When they were finally together—and he never doubted that eventuality—he would ensure their house was properly secured.

A hallway led to the kitchen with a sitting room to the right, an office on the left. The kitchen was pleasant but dated. They would update it together, Machota decided, not that he was particularly interested in kitchens but the reno would be a project they could share.

It occurred to him that the house had much more to do with her recently deceased brother, Bryce, than it did with Jean. For Jean, he imagined, this place was no more than a campsite. There were piles of official papers on the kitchen table—her mother's will and death certificate, letters to two banks seeking to close accounts, forms from a stock broker and an accountant.

He climbed narrow stairs to the master bedroom. A masculine air overwhelmed by a mustiness that indicated no one had been in here for a while. Bryce's room, he surmised, untouched since his death.

Jean occupied the tiny guest bedroom. Her scent hung in the air. He inhaled it. Yes, this is where she existed, no question. He went through her clothes closet, found the brown Mountie tunic preserved in a plastic bag. What did Jean think? That maybe someday she would rejoin the force again and all would be forgiven?

Dream on, wonderful Jean, he thought, seated on the bed. That was never going to happen. He stretched out on the brightly flowered duvet, imagining her beside him, naked, luxuriating in the image of the two of them here together.

He opened his pants and took out his cock. It was already hard just thinking about her.

He began to stroke himself. Wouldn't take long.

Jean, he thought. Ah, Jean, Jean…

11

As soon as she entered the house, Jean sensed that something wasn't right. Someone had been inside. It was as if the air had been moved around in ways that it shouldn't have been moved. The documents on the table in the kitchen looked much the same as she had left them. Except they weren't the same.

She searched the ground floor, found nothing amiss, and then went upstairs. When she entered the bedroom, she saw what had been left behind on the bed. Her stomach twisted in revulsion. The bastard had broken in, come into her bedroom, jerked off, and then left the evidence for her viewing pleasure.

She took deep breaths, thought about the police and then decided against calling. They could take DNA samples that would put Machota in the bedroom. But the results would take weeks if not months in the face of Machota's assertions that they had had consensual sex.

No, the police weren't the answer, she decided, stripping off the sheets and carrying them down to the basement laundry room and dumping them in the washing machine. She knew she shouldn't, she knew this was part of his sick game designed to play with her head, but nonetheless she felt invaded, assaulted in much the same way Machota had assaulted her in Afghanistan.

The police baton remained on the counter against the backsplash where she had left it. The Ruger .45 semi-automatic was in the drawer below the counter. She removed it and set it behind a wicker basket filled with bread and crackers, within easier reach.

She checked the door locks. Anyone with a couple of picks could defeat the deadbolts. She phoned a locksmith. The Kwikset double-cylinder deadbolt was the most burglar-proof lock available, he told her. Of course, he cautioned, the best lock was only as good as the door to which it was attached. The locksmith was backed up. He could schedule her in a couple of weeks. That was fine, Jean said.

She began to feel better. She had taken action to protect herself. All to the good. Even so, Machota had entered her space in the most disgusting way. If he would do this, she concluded, he wasn't going to stop. He would continue to harass her. The question was this: what was she going to do, other than change the sheets?

———————

Reagan hung in until 10 p.m.

Then she became fed up with what Machota had termed "a stakeout," and called him. "How much longer am I supposed to do this?"

"Until I tell you to leave," came the terse reply.

"Adam, nothing's happening. It's late. She's not coming out."

"Stay put until I tell you otherwise." Machota hung up the phone.

"Shit!" Reagan exclaimed. That bastard, she thought. And he was a bastard, no question. An attractive bastard, a bastard who knew how to push the right buttons.

But a bastard.

Reagan had parked the rental car at a Mill Street strip mall with a view of Jean Whitlock's house. At least it was the house where Machota said she lived. Other than briefly glimpsing her through a restaurant window, Reagan had not laid eyes on this woman. What was his interest in her, anyway? Okay, Jean Whitlock was the focus of this mysterious undercover operation. What was that all about? The whole thing was kind of weird, if she was being truthful with herself. But then Machota was kind of weird. Not kind of weird, she corrected.

Weird.

Reagan got out of the car and lit a cigarette, inhaling deeply. That calmed her. She kept telling herself she was going to quit, and she was, each time she finished a cigarette. Whatever. She sure as shit wasn't going to quit tonight. She leaned against the car, dragging on the cigarette.

Weird.

Not to mention a bastard. How did she always get mixed up with the bastards? Weren't there any nice guys out there, somewhere? Guys who weren't so weird?

"You don't have another one of those, do you?"

The voice startled her. She turned to see a tall man coming toward her. In the way Reagan by default assessed members of the opposite sex, she immediately slotted this guy into the Kind of Attractive category.

Rugged. A little older than she might have liked. But attractive.

"Sure," she said. "No problem." She handed him the pack.

"I'm trying to quit," the tall man said, extracting a cigarette from the pack and handing it back to her.

"Aren't we all," Reagan said with a quick smile. In this little town on a quiet residential street this guy didn't look too much like an axe murderer, as her mother used to describe men.

"The next thing I'm going to have to trouble you for is a light."

"You really are trying to quit," Reagan said.

"That's me, a quitter." The tall man grinned. "Over and over again."

Reagan laughed and said, "I shouldn't be encouraging you."

But she fished out the Bic lighter from her jeans and applied the thin flame to the end of his cigarette.

"Many thanks," he said.

"I hope I'm not corrupting you," Reagan said.

"I'm beyond corruption at this point," he said.

"Not too far beyond, I hope."

"Not so far," he said. He pulled on his cigarette and then gave her what she was certain was—her mother again—the once over. She got the impression he liked what he saw; but when they saw her, most men liked what they saw. Not that it did her much good when it came to attracting bastards like Adam Machota.

"Are you okay?" he asked.

She gave him a fleeting smile. "Why shouldn't I be?"

"I saw you alone and wanted to make sure you're all right," he said.

"I didn't want to smoke in the car, so I pulled in here," Reagan said, pleased with herself at how fast she could come up with an excuse for hanging out late at night.

"What's your name?" the tall man asked.

"Reagan," she answered. "Reagan Elliott."

"Nice to meet you, Reagan."

"Nice to meet you, too—well, I don't know your name, do I?"

"Mickey," the tall man said.

"Mouse?"

The tall man laughed. "No. Dann. Mickey Dann."

12

Splotches of color on the trees crowding either side of Highway 25 signified the turning of the season. Autumn arriving gently on caressing winds, reminding Jean as she drove north of time passing, time wasted wondering what to do with the rest of her life.

Residential developments—townhouses, condos, sprawling mega-mansions—exploding east and west thus far had less enthusiasm for a northern march. But overgrown fields abutting the highway awaited the developer's excavators. Civilization was coming, delayed for a short time.

Acton straggled into view. Jean came along the all-but-deserted Main Street to the single downtown light. She turned right onto Queen Street, maneuvering past earth-moving machinery gouging at the roadway.

The Bethel Christian Reformed Church stood further along the street. She turned into the church parking lot, swinging around to the back so that the SUV was out of sight. There was as yet no sign of Desiree, but then Jean had purposely arrived early.

Fir trees lined the north side of the parking lot adjacent to a swath of patchy grass separating the church grounds from the small shopping mall next door. Jean positioned herself behind the trees so that she had a view of the parking lot, and then waited.

And waited.

The descending sun spread long shadows across the parking lot, washing the church in crimson and gold, the heavens beckoning.

Jean stayed earthbound, resisting heaven's call, feeling increasingly cramped in her position behind the trees. She checked her watch. It was after eight. What had happened to Desiree? And for that matter where were her prospective blackmailers?

She rose, stretched, and then withdrew her cellphone in hopes Desiree had called, and she'd somehow missed it.

But no one had.

"Hey." She turned to see a teenage boy coming toward her from the direction of the mall.

"Yes?" she called back to him.

"There's a lady in a car," the teenager said, concern etched on his pale face. "I'm not sure if she's sleeping or what. Do you mind taking a look?"

"Where's the car?" Jean asked. Cold fear played along her spine.

"Back here," the boy said, jerking a thumb behind him.

Jean went past him. "Stay where you are, okay?" The boy nodded and didn't move. A familiar-looking Audi half hidden behind a steel dumpster, was at the far end of the parking area.

Jean reached the car, steeled herself, and then bent down to peer in the passenger-side window. Through the tinted glass she could make out a form slumped over the wheel.

Jean tried the Audi's handle. The door opened. Jean leaned inside. "Desiree," Jean called out. Desiree did not answer. Desiree's head was thrown forward, her cheek pressed against the wheel of the Audi. One of Desiree's sightless eyes studied Jean's grim face. Blood from a ragged throat wound spilled down the front of her blouse and ran down over her jeans, and across the seat and the floor.

———————

The teenage boy remained frozen in place at the far end of the parking lot. He had short bristly brown hair, and he wore a backpack. Typical teenager around these parts, Jean thought walking back to him.

He began to tremble, sensing something was very wrong. "It's all right," Jean said. "Tell me your name."

"It's Mason," said the boy in a breaking voice. "Is she—"

"I'm going to call the police," Jean said, keeping her voice calm. "They are going to want to talk to you. Are you okay with that?"

"I was just going home," he said.

"I know. This is terrible that you're involved. But you have to stay here. Understand?"

"Am I in trouble?" he asked, his eyes blank with fear.

"Of course not. You did the right thing."

Jean pulled her cellphone from her pocket and was about to dial 911 when she saw the car pull into the church parking lot below her. The car turned into one of the spaces at the side of the lot facing the street and came to a stop.

Jean paused with the phone in her hand, keeping her eyes on the car, waiting to see who got out. For what seemed endless minutes, no one did.

Then the driver's-side door opened and a figure stepped out.

In the fading light, Adam Machota looked around, taking in his surroundings. His gaze fell upon Jean standing atop the grassy embankment with the cell-phone in her hand.

When he saw her, he smiled and waved. A victory smile? Jean wondered.

Then he got into the car and drove out of the lot.

13

Mason's distraught parents came to collect their son after he had been interviewed by Halton police officers. The police had come in force minutes after Jean made the 911 call, local cops trying not to look shocked by the sight of a dead woman bleeding all over the front seat of her Audi.

An ambulance appeared and shortly after that a big red fire truck came screaming in, all the emergency organizations in the area racing to the scene.

There was nothing any of them could do, of course. As much as they milled about chatting to one another—what did authority figures at crime scenes find to talk about in hushed whispers? Jean always wondered—Desiree Whitlock remained dead.

If Halton detective Glen Petrusiak was surprised to see Jean, he did a good job of hiding it.

Mickey Dann was not with Petrusiak. Instead, he had a different partner, a young, dark-eyed woman he introduced as Indira Kobus. She silently shook Jean's hand. Her dark eyes said plenty, Jean thought, ablaze with intelligence.

By now the area had been cordoned off with yellow police tape. A small crowd had gathered beyond the tape.

Petrusiak gazed into the car. "Shit," Jean heard him say to Indira Kobus. "It's the mayor's wife."

Indira Kobus maintained a professional demeanor. Instead of showing emotion, the detective kneeled to inspect the dead woman for herself. "Yes," was all she commented after straightening.

Petrusiak swirled and strode back to where Jean stood with a couple of uniformed officers. "What the hell," he said.

"I know," she said.

"You know?" Petrusiak snapped. "What do you know? What are you doing here?"

Indira Kobus hovered behind him. "We better phone this in," she said quietly.

"Have you called the mayor?" Petrusiak demanded to Jean.

Jean shook her head. "I haven't called anyone."

"Jesus," Petrusiak said. "This is going to cause a shitstorm. How the hell did this happen?"

"She wanted me to meet her here," Jean answered, trying to keep the story as simple as she could without giving too much away just yet.

"In a goddamn strip mall in Acton? Why the hell would she want you to do that?"

"In the church parking lot, actually," Jean amended. "She said she was being blackmailed."

"Who? Who was blackmailing her?"

"I don't think she knew for certain. That's why she came—to find out what these people had on her."

"What have you got to do with any of this?"

"Desiree didn't want to do this alone. She asked me to be with her."

"You? Why would she ask you?" Petrusiak demanded.

She caught Indira Kobus's dark eyes riveted to her.

"I used to be a cop. I would know how to handle the situation."

"But you didn't handle the situation," Petrusiak said.

"I got to the church early and waited. She didn't show up at eight when she was supposed to. Then Mason came along, the boy who spotted a car behind the dumpster. That's when I found her."

"You have no idea who she was supposed to meet here?"

"No."

"And no one showed up?"

Jean thought of the brief glimpse she got of Adam Machota before he drove off again. Then she said, "No."

Despite repeated attempts, no one could reach Mayor Jock Whitlock on either his home phone or his mobile. Thus, there was surprise when he suddenly showed up. By then the growing crowd had been pushed back out of the strip mall, down onto the church grounds. A staging area had been established with a tent that served as a mobile operations center.

Beneath the glare of floodlights set up by the Ontario Provincial Police crime scene unit that Petrusiak had called in, techies swarmed around Desiree's car in their white Tyvek suits. Under the lights, they appeared like slow-moving spacemen adrift on an alien planet.

The chief of police, Walt Dunnell, was also present, a big, plump man with large, sleepy eyes, a comb over that emphasized his baldness and a propensity for puffing out his chest and looking important, possibly to hide the fact that his troops thought him dumb as a doornail, a perception he did little to counter.

Jock was pale and grim-faced as he made his way across the parking lot, accompanied by his assistant, Grace Travis. Although Jean had spoken many times on the phone to Grace, she hadn't actually seen her since returning to Milton. Grace hadn't changed much over the years, still the tiny, birdlike embodiment of local power's quiet, dependable servant. Grace held all the mayor's secrets, held them tight.

Trailing behind Grace and Jock came a sleek, white-haired operator named Eddie Fitzpatrick. Eddie—no one called him Edward—had been Jock's attorney since anyone could remember. The commonly held wisdom was that Eddie Fitzpatrick had, over the years, single-handedly kept Jock out of jail. If you were in trouble in the Toronto area, you went to Eddie. He also represented Del Caulder, Milton's most prominent developer. However, Eddie had been unable to get Del bail, and thus he remained a guest of the Maplehurst Prison in Milton awaiting trial on charges ranging from forcible confinement to money laundering and fraud.

Jean watched Jock shake hands with Chief Dunnell while Petrusiak and the sharp-eyed Indira Kobus hovered in the background. Not the way it should be at a crime scene, Jean thought, but political reality in these circumstances.

Jock made a move toward the Audi. The chief blocked him. "You can't go up there, Jock," he said gently.

"Jesus Christ," Jock said.

As this happened, Grace thrust herself at Jean, wrapping her in an awkward embrace. "This is so terrible," she murmured. "Beyond words."

"Yes," Jean said.

Grace pulled away to focus on Jean. "Are you all right? I understand you found Desiree."

"I'm okay, Grace, thanks," Jean said.

"This is just so awful," Grace said in a mournful voice. "So terrible, terrible."

"They were trying to get hold of Jock," Jean said.

Immediately, Grace became guarded. "He was out of the office," she said carefully.

Eddie Fitzpatrick joined them, the scent of his aftershave preceding him. Ordinarily, Eddie could flash a smile that lit a courtroom and swayed a jury. But not tonight. Tonight, he adopted the sober countenance of a man present at a tragedy.

"Jean, it's been a long time," Eddie said in his distinctive, rumbling baritone. "I'm sorry we meet again under these circumstances."

"Hello, Eddie," Jean said.

Eddie flashed a quick smile, and then, almost as an afterthought, in case anyone might need an explanation as to why Jock would bring his lawyer to his wife's murder: "Jock asked me to be with him at this terrible time."

Jean thought: Jock receives the news of his wife's murder and immediately calls his lawyer? But that was all she had time to think before Jock himself was throwing his arms around her and burying his face in her shoulder. "Jean," he said, "God, Jean."

"This is terrible, terrible," Jean heard Grace repeating like a mantra.

"Terrible," echoed Eddie Fitzpatrick.

Jock loosened his grip on Jean so he could guide her away to the side of the church. He faced her, his face in shadows, showing nothing. He said, "What have you told the police?"

Not the first question you should ask after your wife has been murdered, she thought. Aloud, she said, "I told them what happened."

"They say Desiree asked you to meet her out here."

"That's right."

"Do you know anything about twenty-five thousand dollars?"

"Yes," Jean said.

Jock closed his eyes. "Jesus Christ," he said. Then he opened them again and asked, "Did you tell them that I asked you to follow her?"

Jean shook her head. For some reason that seemed to relieve Jock. "I don't think there's any reason to tell them now," he said. It was not a request.

"I'm not going to lie, Jock."

"I'm not asking you to lie. I'm suggesting it's not necessary to say anything. Christ, I can't believe you did this without telling me."

"There wasn't time," Jean said. "She said someone was trying to blackmail her. The twenty-five thousand was supposed to be a down payment."

"The police say it's not in the car."

Before Jean could respond to that, shadows loomed out of the light thrown off by the crime scene. Petrusiak, followed by Indira Kobus. "Mister Mayor," Petrusiak said in a formal voice. "We need you to come with us."

Jock looked suddenly nervous. "What do you need me for? Have you talked to Eddie?"

"We don't need to talk to Eddie, we need to talk to you," Petrusiak said. "Would you follow Detective Kobus, please? She and another officer will take you back to Milton."

"I need to talk to Eddie," Jock said.

"Mr. Fitzpatrick is waiting for you by one of the police vehicles."

"Come with me please, Mr. Mayor." Crisply delivered orders from Indira Kobus.

"I don't like this," Jock muttered. "I need to talk to Eddie."

But he followed Detective Kobus across the parking lot, leaving Jean alone with Petrusiak.

"What was all that about?" he asked, turning to her.

"He's just found out his wife has been murdered. He's pretty upset."

"Funny, he doesn't seem all that upset," Petrusiak said.

Jean agreed with him but said nothing.

"What do you think? Was she screwing around?" Petrusiak asked.

"I don't know for sure, but she was certainly worried."

Petrusiak nodded in the direction of the departing mayor. "Do you think he suspected something?"

"I don't know," Jean said, the first lie out of her mouth this evening—the lie she said she would not tell.

Petrusiak gave her a narrow look. "Are you telling me everything?"

"Everything I know," Jean said. "Which isn't much."

"Did Jock ask you to lie?"

"No, he didn't," Jean replied.

"Do you know who might want to kill Desiree?"

"I don't know her well enough to answer that," Jean said.

"What about Jock?"

"What about him?"

"Would he kill her?"

"Is that what you're thinking?" Knowing that was exactly what he was thinking. What she would be thinking if she was the investigating officer.

"Tell me." Petrusiak in demanding voice. "Would he?"

"No, I don't think he would," Jean said.

And then immediately wondered if she hadn't just told another lie.

14

Machota was right, Moose Haggerty thought. The lock was shit. If you knew what you were doing, it was nothing to spring it.

Moose knew what he was doing.

Holding the can of wood alcohol in one hand, he eased the door open, calling out, "Hello, anyone home?"

No answer. Machota, thankfully, had been right about that, too. He withdrew the balaclava from the side pocket of his windbreaker and pulled it over his head before stepping inside. Machota said there were no security cameras. But better to be safe than sorry.

He closed and locked the door, turning to survey the interior.

A small, neat house, cottage-like. He could live in a place like this, big enough for him to spread out, but not a problem to keep clean. A shame to destroy such a nice little house. But that was his job, wasn't it? He didn't create things, he destroyed them.

A kind of creation in itself, he believed.

He had no trouble finding the stairs to the basement, the best location for what he had in mind. It was very much as he expected. A low-ceilinged space filled with lots of junk—a rusted bicycle, a couple of discarded sofas, straight-back chairs piled on top of one another, odds and ends of lumber, and, even better, piles of old newspapers not far from a counter jammed with paint cans and brushes.

Perfect.

He set the wood alcohol on the counter. There was enough shit here to ignite a fire without it. But the alcohol was more reliable and effective. He pulled the ignitor chord out of his backpack, a time-delay device fashioned with black powder and wrapped in a thin layer of asphalt coating. He had used it before with excellent results—except the last time. That miscalculation, the inattention to detail, had landed him in prison. But he was smarter now, he told himself, more experienced. Not likely to make the same mistakes again.

At least, that was his intention.

If he wanted to be sure to cover every possibility, he should establish multiple ignition points around the basement. But that would take more time and if one of those points failed to ignite, it became evidence for fire investigators.

That's what got him into trouble the last time. Lesson learned.

He set the timer, adjusted the chord so that it couldn't be seen unless you closely inspected the counter.

Yes, he thought. This would work. He was in the midst of congratulating himself for a professional job well done when he heard the front door open.

———

Jean came in, anxious to crawl into bed, put the night's events out of her mind, try not to think that she was partially responsible for Desiree's death, that if she had been more attentive, Jock's wife would still be alive.

Jean closed the door and as soon as she did, she sensed …

Something.

She stood stock still in the entry hall, not breathing. Listening.

From below, movement. Not much. Hardly a scrape.

But movement.

The basement stairs were off the hall, between her and the kitchen—where she had placed the gun and the baton. She needed to get to the kitchen.

Get there fast.

She started along the hall—but not fast enough. A bulky figure abruptly blocked her way. A big man, his face covered by a balaclava that transformed him into the monster from a bad teen slasher movie.

Except she was no teen.

The balaclava-clad movie monster started when he saw her. That gave Jean the opening she needed—her booted foot shot into the monster's groin.

The monster howled, no monster, just an asshole, balls on fire as he crumpled over.

If the violent events had unfolded as they were supposed to, she would have had a second opening, allowing her to knee the asshole in the face. Except the asshole recovered a lot faster than she anticipated, and the knee aimed for a face instead struck hard shoulder, sending bone-crunching pain shooting through her body.

The pain slowed her just enough to give the asshole-turned-monster-again the time he needed to smash her face. Her nose burst, spraying blood, as she tumbled back. Before she could right herself, the reinvigorated monster charged, knocking into her, sending her sprawling to the floor.

The monster clambered over her, headed for the door, but she retained the presence of mind to grasp him at the knees, and that, coupled with his desperate forward trajectory, caused him to lose balance and slam down hard onto the floor.

Jean jumped to her feet, lurching for the kitchen, reaching the counter an instant before he was on her—surprising her again with his speed and ability to make a fast recovery. His fist pounded into the small of her back, knocking the air out of her. She fell to the floor and that made her vulnerable enough that he was able to get off a kick to her ribs and then a second blow smashing her face.

Stars exploded into a searing brightness that swiftly descended into the darkness with which she was only too familiar. As she faded, she could hear in the distance the thump of departing feet, a door opening and then slamming shut.

The monster escaping.

15

At first, Reagan didn't think she was going to do anything.

But then the heat suddenly rose up and enveloped her. She screamed, slamming against him, and screamed again before collapsing.

He rolled her onto her back and came into her, going deep, filling her and the next thing he was groaning and then grunting, coming inside her.

Reagan snuggled against him. "My good Samaritan."

"Not that good."

"Very good," Reagan said, her hand caressing. "Impressive."

"I just phoned to make sure you were all right," he said.

"I'm better now," she said, her hand at work.

"I need a minute," he said.

"I need a pee," she said, bounding out of bed. He admired her body all over again as she sashayed into the bathroom and closed the door.

Mickey lay back, refusing to allow his cop's innate suspicion of everything and everyone to get in the way of enjoying the evening. What was this? Good luck? A fortuitous meeting? Yeah, right. But then he immediately dismissed the cynicism gathering in the back of his mind. They had met. They were attracted to one another. They had ended in bed. It happens. Don't overthink it.

Before he could worry much more, she was back, bouncing onto the bed, mashing her mouth against his. They were about to move it up another notch when his cellphone began to make noises.

"What's that?" Reagan asked, coming up for air.

"My phone," Mickey said. He reached for it on the bedside table.

"Do you have to?" She was rubbing her body against him and he almost decided not to answer. Then he saw who it was.

"I'd better take this."

Reagan made a disappointed face and fell away while Mickey sat up swiping open his phone. "Hey," he said.

Jean said, "I've just been attacked."

"Where?"

"In my house. A guy in a balaclava. He was waiting for me when I came in."

"Okay," Mickey said. "Give me a few minutes and I'll be over."

"Thanks, Mickey."

Mickey put his phone down. "I have to go."

"A girlfriend?" Reagan gave him the sort of co-quettish look that suggested no girlfriend could ever match her allure.

"A cop friend. Well, a former-cop friend."

"You're a cop?"

Mickey grinned. "Didn't I mention that?"

"No, you didn't," Reagan said. She moved away from him.

"Do you have a problem with that?"

"I don't know," Reagan said. "I've never been with a cop before."

"We're just like everyone else, only better."

"Is that so?"

"I'm a police officer. I can't tell a lie."

"Yeah. Right."

"It's true," Mickey said.

Reagan stretched on the bed, displaying her nude body. "Perhaps you'd better provide a demonstration."

"Yes," Mickey said, positioning himself over her. "I think we have time for that."

———————

Jean was still trying to stop her nose bleeding when Mickey got to her place. The side of her face was on fire, ribs aching from where her assailant had kicked her.

"You didn't see who it was?" Mickey asked once she had more or less outlined the sequence of events that had unfolded when she unlocked the door to her house.

She shook her head. "Like I said, he was wearing a balaclava."

"No idea how he got in?"

"It looks like he picked the lock."

"Is it that easy to get in here?"

"It's a lousy lock."

"Could it have been Machota?"

"Too big."

"Hard to believe it was just a random break-and-enter," Mickey said.

"I don't think it was," Jean said.

"Was he after something? Is anything missing?"

"I don't know, I haven't had time to look around. He came up from the cellar."

"What's in the cellar?"

"Nothing," Jean said.

"Let me take a quick look around, and then I'll drive you over to emergency."

"I'm fine," Jean said.

"No, you're not," Mickey replied. "Come on, Jean. You know better. After something like this you should get checked out."

"I'm upset with myself," she said. "Maybe I don't want the world to know I couldn't handle something I should have been able to handle."

"Let me look downstairs, and then I'll drive you to the hospital," Mickey said.

"You look, I'll call my doctor. Maybe she can see me. A little more discreet."

"I'll be right back," Mickey said.

He found the light switch at the top of the stairs and went down into the cellar. All sorts of shit down here, he quickly surmised. Almost impossible to say if anything was missing. Still, why would a burglar bother with a cellar?

Unless it wasn't a burglary. It was something else.

He stood over the counter containing the empty paint cans. It took his eyes a moment to adjust to the uncertain light from the overhead bulb. Something black and shiny seemed out of place. He picked it up, wondering what the hell that was for. It looked like a piece of hardened asphalt. Amazing the shit that got stored away in basements and then forgotten.

He threw the asphalt piece back on the counter.

16

Reagan, dead-tired, looking forward to a long sleep, came into her room at the Best Western to find Moose with Machota. Neither of them looked happy to see her.

"Where the hell have you been?" Machota demanded.

"You told me to stay put and watch the house," Reagan said.

"You didn't see me?" Moose asked.

"Was I supposed to see you?"

"I was in the house," Moose said. "I didn't see any sign of you."

"Well, I was there," Reagan said defensively, sitting on the bed and removing her shoes.

"Bullshit," Moose said.

"The point is," Machota said, "Moose was in the house when Jean came back. You didn't spot her, Reagan?"

"No, I didn't," Reagan said. She thought to herself: *Shit.* "I didn't know Moose was going to be at the house—which someone should have told me. And I didn't see her go in."

"You were asleep," accused Moose.

"I wasn't asleep," Reagan protested. True enough. She was in bed, she thought fleetingly, but she certainly wasn't sleeping. "Listen, no one told me shit." She pointed a finger at Machota. "You told me to sit tight. I sat tight. You didn't tell me anything about Moose. You didn't give me any idea when this woman I'm supposed to be watching was coming home. If this had been set up better, if I'd known about Moose, then I could have watched the front. But even if I had seen her, how the hell was I supposed to warn Moose?"

Machota rose and kissed her mouth. Then he slapped her face. "Don't ever talk to me like that. Understand?"

He raised his hand again. She cringed away and said, "Yes, Jesus, I understand."

Machota lowered his hand and took a deep breath. "Okay, we got a little off track here. Communication may not have been what it should be. I blame myself for that. Next time I'll make sure we co-ordinate things better."

Machota addressed Moose. "The important thing is you accomplished your mission, Moose. That's what counts. You did what you were supposed to do."

"Yeah, I got in there all right, but I almost didn't get out. This is one tough bitch, let me tell you."

"I know how tough she is," Machota said.

"Remind me again why we're doing this," Moose said.

"All you need to know, you're involved in an undercover operation designed to bring down a rogue RCMP member."

"This Jean Whitlock being the rogue member in question?"

"That's correct," Machota said.

"I don't want to end up in jail over this," Moose said.

"You're working for me," Machota said. "I've got your backs, both of you."

"I hope so, because we are about to unleash some serious shit," Moose said.

"What kind of shit is that?" Reagan wanted to know.

Machota shot her a look. "You look tired, Reagan. Why don't you take a shower, get cleaned up? After that we can get something to eat."

"Sure," Reagan said. She got off the bed.

Machota watched her as she disappeared into the bathroom.

Wondering.

———————

The room wasn't much but at least the shower worked. Reagan could stay anywhere as long as there was a comfortable bed and a shower. Good thing that was all that she needed, given her current circumstances.

She turned her face into the water gushing from the shower head, still angry at Machota for slapping her. He'd never done that before.

Bastard.

But then she already knew that about him. She hadn't anticipated the hitting part, though. The part that transformed him from bastard into a dangerous, violent bastard. No way was she going to put up with that shit.

Moose might be dumb enough to believe Machota's bullshit story about an undercover operation. But she wasn't. There was no undercover operation as far as she could see. This was a guy out for some kind of crazy revenge. And from the sound of what she heard in the other room, it was about to get a whole lot crazier.

Reagan ran the crappy little bar of soap provided by the hotel over her body. She thought of Mickey Dann and that produced a tingle of warmth. Not a bad guy as it turned out. A cop but not a bad guy, particularly in bed.

Still, he was a cop and given her circumstances, that wasn't good. Or was it? The more she thought about it, the more Reagan decided that a cop might work in her best interest. Mickey Dann could be her ace in the hole if Machota got out of control again. After all, a guy who would hit her, pretty much unprovoked, what else was he capable of?

Just about anything.

Reagan allowed the spray to wash away the soap before turning off the taps and stepping out of the tub, feeling better, less vulnerable. More in control. She had a plan involving a cop named Mickey Dann.

Mickey, her hero. Mickey, the guy who just might save her skin.

17

Jean came awake, blind, disoriented, in a dream, the loud, intrusive sound of an alarm.

It took a moment to realize this was no dream. The smoke alarm was sounding loudly, insistently.

She rolled off the bed, trying to remember the training she received when finding herself trapped in a fire situation. The training she never thought she would have to use. Smoke was full of toxins. Smoke could kill you. Get below the smoke.

Jean dropped to her hands and knees and crawled across the room to the doorway. If she had followed strict protocols, she would have made sure her bedroom door was closed so that the smoke could not easily get in. But who followed protocols when you slept alone? Who closed bedroom doors?

Out in the hallway, the air filled with smoke. Below, she could see flames leaping toward her. The entire ground floor appeared to be ablaze. She retreated back to her bedroom, made sure she closed the door and went to the window on the other side of the room. She opened it and leaned out. Below, the hillside fell off quickly, reinforced by a stone wall abutting the paved drive next door. Jumping from this height could do serious damage.

Now smoke filled the room. She gasped for breath, feeling faint, beginning to lose consciousness. She sank to the floor, dimly thinking where she had read about how long you could last in a smoke-filled room—two minutes? Ten? No more than that.

Dimly she could hear the crackle of flames, feeling light-headed, as though she could fly above it all.

A shape formed out of the smoke. A welcoming presence, she thought, someone to provide solace during her final moments. The shape announced something she couldn't make out and then took on human form lifting her up. No, it wasn't possible, she thought. Nobody could have gotten through the fire.

As she died, she imagined an impossibly heroic outcome, Rhett arriving in the nick of time to save Scarlett from burning Atlanta. She felt herself lifted higher.

Floating into black clouds.

———

Jean became aware of something on her face allowing her to breathe. She opened her eyes, realizing an oxygen mask had been applied by a young man wearing a fireman's helmet that was too big for him.

"There you go," the young fireman said. "Just breathe slowly. Take deep, slow breaths."

Jean did just that, beginning to feel better, her head clearing. Slowly, she sat up, the young fireman keeping the oxygen mask in place. Someone had wrapped a rough blanket around her, before placing her in the back of an ambulance. Outside, she was aware of a flickering light.

"What's that?" she asked.

The young fireman looked confused. "Why, it's your house, ma'am. It's on fire."

Yes, of course, she thought. What else could it be? Her house burning.

She pushed the oxygen mask away so that she could slide out of the ambulance and view for the first time the entire night tableau: glistening yellow fire trucks, police cruisers and ambulances, the platoons of neighbors out to see firefighters training their hoses on the centerpiece of the unfolding drama.

Her house.

The devouring flames sent a great plume of smoke into the night. This old house had managed to stand in Milton since the 1800s, but this old house was no match for the twenty-first century fire that now engulfed it. She held back the urge to break down in tears. Until tonight, she would have said she had lost almost everything in her life.

Now, with the house disappearing before her eyes, she could take the word *almost* out of the sentence.

But she wasn't going to cry. She wasn't going to do that, not in front of all these people. She was tougher than the rest.

Or so she liked to think.

She sensed the young fireman behind her, providing the excuse to turn away from the destruction. "Do you know how I got here?" she asked.

The young fireman had a square, clear face, the prototypical fireman's face, she thought, an image not entirely ruined by the oversized helmet. The face beneath that helmet registered confusion. "Ma'am?"

"I remember someone coming for me, carrying me out of the house."

The young fireman pointed a finger and said, "That gentleman over there. He saved your life."

Jean turned to see Adam Machota approaching, smiling. "How are you doing, Jean? A little smoke inhalation I imagine, but otherwise unscathed."

She looked at him, speechless.

"It was touch and go there for a while," Machota went on. "I didn't think we were going to make it out, but the gods were on our side tonight, I guess, and so here we are."

"This fellow's a damned hero," piped the young fireman.

"I'm just glad I happened to be passing," Machota said. He didn't take his eyes off Jean when he added, "The important thing is you're all right. That's what counts. Right Jean?"

She tried to open her mouth to say something. Anything.

But she couldn't.

18

It's bullshit," Jean said the next day when she met Mickey Dann at Coffee Culture in the Carriage Mall on Main Street.

"That this guy Machota saved your life?" Mickey asked.

"He didn't *save* my life," Jean shot back. "I won't allow myself to think this prick saved my life. He once tried to kill me, for God's sake."

"Well, whatever you may think, he didn't try to kill you this time."

"Something is wrong," Jean said. "What happened doesn't make sense. My house suddenly catches fire in the middle of the night, and Adam Machota just happens to be driving past and sees the flames?"

"That's basically what Machota told fire investigators," Mickey said.

"And how did the fire start in the first place?"

"You think Machota burned down your house?"

"Someone breaks into my place and shortly afterward there's a fire. Kind of convenient, don't you think?"

"Right now, the Fire Marshall's investigators aren't saying anything about the cause," Mickey said. "We're going to have to wait for their report."

"Who knows how long that's going to take."

Mickey looked at his watch.

"Am I keeping you?"

"I've got to meet someone," Mickey said. "But there's no hurry. What are your plans?"

"I don't know," she said with a sigh. "Everything was lost in the fire; not that I had a lot to lose, but the family home since I-don't-know-when is gone. For now, Doris is letting me stay in the apartment over the funeral home."

Mickey stole another glance at his watch. Jean picked up on it. "Okay, now I know you've got to go."

Mickey gave a sheepish smile. "I should get out of here."

"Don't tell me you've got a date."

"An appointment," Mickey corrected.

"Before you go, let me suggest something."

"Sure."

"Machota hired someone to set that fire. I caught the guy as he was coming up from the basement where he had planted some sort of incendiary device."

"That I missed, if that's the case," Mickey interjected.

"We don't know anything for sure, but let's suppose a device was planted. Machota would know when it was triggered. Thus, he could arrange to be present, break into the house and make a heroic show of saving me."

"Look, anything is possible," Mickey said. "But it raises the question: why? If he hates you so much, why not let you perish in the fire?"

"That I don't know," Jean said.

"Unless he really was just passing by, and he really did save your life."

Jean shook her head. "I don't believe it. He's up to something. Playing with me."

"He told the investigators that he's staying at the Best Western here in town. Let me go around and have a talk with him. I can say I'm following up after the fire. See what he has to say for himself."

"I guess it wouldn't hurt," Jean said.

Mickey stood, reaching for his wallet. "It's okay," Jean said. "I've got it."

"Thanks," Mickey said. "I'll be in touch."

"I appreciate this, Mickey."

"Hey, you're buying the coffee."

"You know what I mean," Jean said.

"You don't deserve this shit. I just wish there was more I could do for you."

"You're a shoulder to cry on," Jean said with a smile. "That's something, believe me. Shoulders are in short supply these days."

"Glad to be of service," Mickey said.

"Go off to your date."

"Appointment."

Jean gave him a knowing smile. She watched him go out the door wondering how she felt about him, thinking she could be a teeny bit jealous that he might be meeting another woman. The high school date she could barely remember, had become the guy she could spend more time with under the right circumstances. Not that anything happening lately ever could be categorized as 'right circumstances.'

But had she not learned long ago that a cop should never get involved with another cop? Yes, she was sure she had learned that lesson—the hard way, by being a cop getting involved with a cop.

No, Mickey was the shoulder to cry on, no more than that.

Her phone sounded. She pulled it out of her pocket and swiped it open.

Adam Machota asked, "How are you feeling, Jean? Are you all right?"

"How did you get this number?"

"I've been worried," Machota said. "Frankly, I'm surprised I haven't heard from you."

"Why would you hear from me, Adam?" Jean, trying to keep her voice level, deny him any sense that he might be getting to her.

"Given what I did, Jean, I guess I expected some sort of thank you."

"I don't want you calling me," Jean said. "I want you to leave me alone. I want you out of town and out of my life."

Machota laughed and said, "Well, that's fine thanks, isn't it? I think I deserve better."

"You're not getting shit from me. Do you understand?"

"Jean, I saved your life," Machota said calmly.

"You burned down my house, you bastard." Jean's voice was edged with fury. "I'm going to make you pay. You're going to pay dearly."

"You know what my saving your life indicates to me, Jean?" Machota's voice maintained a preternatural calmness. "It indicates to me that we are destined to be together."

"Go to hell," Jean said.

"I'm probably on my way," Machota said. "I'm going to take you with me. We're going to be together, no matter what. That's a promise."

19

Reagan appeared an hour or so after Mickey got back to his townhouse. It had begun to rain, thunder rumbling across the darkening sky as she pecked him on the cheek and announced, "I'm late."

"It's all right," he said. "I just got home myself. Gave me a chance to clean up the place."

"A messy bachelor life, huh?"

"I gave the maids the week off," Mickey said.

She slipped past him and stopped to survey the living room. "Not bad, but you could use some pictures on the wall."

"I keep telling myself," he agreed. "But then work keeps getting in the way."

"Bringing down the bad guys," she said, swaying across the room.

Reagan wore a short leather skirt that emphasized the length and shape of her legs. He made himself keep his eyes off those leather-clad hips.

"Can I get you some wine?"

"Sure. Why not?"

"White? Red?"

"You don't have any whiskey, do you?"

He gave her a look. "My kind of woman. Dewar's?"

"Straight," she said.

She trailed him into the kitchen. "I didn't know if I'd hear from you again," she said.

"No? What made you think I wouldn't call?" He withdrew a bottle of Dewar's Scotch from an overhead cupboard.

"You know, you pick up a girl parked at the side of the road. One-night stand."

He grinned, put the scotch down and kissed her. "Never crossed my mind," he said.

She put her arms around him. "I like you. I never thought I'd like a cop, but I like you."

"Cops can be likable."

"Apparently," she said, and then twisted her mouth against his. Her hand was between his legs. "I can't stay too long."

"How long?"

"Long enough," she said.

———————

After they finished, they lay together on the living room floor. "Comfortable?"

She smiled at him and said, "I'm in your arms. How could I not be comfortable?"

He liked that. "I don't know anything about you," he said.

"I don't know anything about you," she replied.

"Not that much to tell. I was born in Milton, went to high school here, became a cop in Toronto. Didn't like it. Came back here to wonder what I'm doing with my life."

"Married?"

"At one point, yeah. It didn't last very long. What about you?"

"Am I married?"

"Are you?"

Quick smile. "Not married. No."

"Boyfriend?"

"An asshole."

"Doesn't sound like much of a boyfriend. Is he from Milton?"

She laughed. "Are you kidding?" She ran her hand along his chest. "Only the nice guys are from Milton."

"You're not from around here." It was a statement of fact.

"Hardly. I've never been here before. I only came here because of him."

"What's your boyfriend doing here?"

"Business, he says."

"What kind of business?"

"The kind of business he doesn't tell me a whole lot about."

"He doesn't sound like someone you should be with."

"No?" She kissed him lightly on the mouth. "Who do you think I should be with?"

"I might have a couple of suggestions."

"A couple?" She kissed him again.

"One or two."

She pulled away a bit, smiling. "You're very nice, too nice. I wish I had met you earlier."

"I get nervous when a woman starts calling me nice."

"It's a compliment, believe me." She pulled further away to lean back against the sofa. "To tell you the truth, I'm feeling kind of trapped."

"This guy you're with. Is he abusive?"

She hesitated before she said, "He can be, yeah."

"Then that's it. You should get out of it."

"Easier said than done."

"Can I help?"

"You're helping just by being here," she said, kissing him again.

"I'm a cop, remember? I can do more if you need more."

She began stroking him. "For now, maybe you could do something with this."

"With a little help," he said.

"How much help do you need?" she said.

"Not much," he said.

"I can see that," she said. "But here, this might make it easier."

And it did.

————

Several hundred yards from Mickey's townhouse, Moose Haggarty got out of his car to stretch his legs and light a cigarette.

It had pretty much stopped raining. The roadway in front of him under street lights remained slick and shiny. He took another drag, hearing the rumble of thunder accompanied by the odd flash of lightning. It was enough to make him think that it would be his damn luck to be hit by lightning in this shitass town doing things that could land him in prison for a long time.

He didn't trust Machota, doubted he was involved in any undercover operation, and now he wondered about Reagan. Two hours ago, she had arrived at the townhouse where she was greeted by a guy who drew her inside and then closed the door.

What would you do to Reagan Elliott if you had two hours alone with her? Not hard to imagine, Moose thought.

How would Machota react to the news of Reagan visiting a new friend? Also, not hard to imagine. After all, if Machota trusted Reagan, Moose wouldn't be following her, would he?

His cellphone sounded, interrupting his reverie. Fishing it out of his pocket, he saw that it was Machota. Not the person he wanted to talk to right now. Nonetheless, he swiped it open.

"Hey, chief. What's up?"

"Where are you?" Machota demanded.

Moose hesitated before he said, "On Main Street."

"Where is Reagan?"

"Shopping as far as I know."

"I've been trying to get hold of her."

"I don't know what you think she's doing, but what she's actually doing—"

"Okay, I don't need any of your smartass shit," Machota snapped.

"I hadn't even got to the smartass shit part, chief," Moose said. He enjoyed turning Machota's crank. Not hard to do, as it turned out. Machota could put him back in jail; the least Moose could do was make his life as miserable as possible.

Machota said, "Get your ass back here."

"Yes, chief," Moose said in his most obsequious voice.

Machota hung up. Interesting, Moose thought to himself as he shoved the cellphone in his pocket, he had gone to bat for Reagan. Spur-of-the-moment decision, maybe having a lot to do with the fact he wasn't a goddamn snitch. For anyone. Certainly not for the Mounties. Also, he kind of liked Reagan. He didn't like Machota hitting her. He didn't like Machota.

Down the street, the front door of the townhouse opened and Reagan stepped into view. She turned when the guy came out and put his arms around her. They kissed as a cab pulled up. Reagan drew away from the guy, smiled, and then dashed down the steps and into the cab.

The guy went back inside as the cab drove off. Now on top of everything else that was screwed up in his life, there was what in Moose's estimation was the worst kind of trouble.

Woman trouble.

20

The front page of Milton's weekly newspaper, the *Champion*, was devoted to the fiery destruction of the historic James Street house, the town's first church, accompanied by a photograph of the structure enveloped in flames.

Jean read the story, drinking morning coffee in the tiny kitchen in the musty apartment above the funeral home. The apartment faced James Street so Jean didn't have to stare at the burned-out shell of her house and be reminded of all that had been lost.

Ancient furniture draped in faded, flowered upholstery clashed with equally faded, flowered wallpaper. A dozen coffins of varying sizes were propped against one wall, awaiting the dead. Dusty urns crowded a mahogany dining table near an ugly brick fireplace, perhaps the height of 1950s fashion. The faint smell of stale cigar smoke permeated the apartment, lingering from the days when her father used to sneak up here to take a puff or two before swearing to his wife that he never smoked cigars.

The *Champion* story was accurate as far as it went, except for the part about the unidentified good Samaritan passing on Mill Street who saw the fire and rushed to the aide of former RCMP Corporal Jean Whitlock.

"If that gentleman hadn't happened along, I believe we would have had a fatality on our hands," fire chief Bill Hamilton told the *Champion*.

Well, the passerby wasn't a passerby, he wasn't unidentified, and if he saved her life it was because he put her life in jeopardy in the first place. Reading the story made her furious all over again. At the same time, she felt helpless. If Machota would burn down her house to make a point, what wasn't he capable of? This time, he had decided to keep her alive.

But what about the next time?

She tossed the paper to one side. This is what it had all come to, the desert upon which the misspent pieces of her life had exhausted themselves. Let's see, she was—well—fortyish, was the best way to put it, alone, unmarried, no prospects, holed up among the coffins and the urns atop a funeral home, the dead in the basement anxious for her to join them, Adam Machota eagerly arranging passage.

She had to stop thinking like this, she told herself; somehow, she must pull herself out of her funk. Easier said than done after your home has burned to the ground and unchecked evil has arrived in town.

The question she had to answer for herself was this: was she going to allow the evil represented by Adam Machota to destroy her life?

Presumably the answer was no. If she were to survive, she would have to act. No one would do anything about Machota. There was only one person who could stop him.

She was that person.

21

Mickey drove to the Best Western Hotel north of the 401.

He parked and entered the hotel's lobby. A plump woman with short gray hair was behind the reception desk. "Hello there, Mrs. McQueen," he said. "Remember me?"

Mrs. McQueen looked up from the computer screen that was causing her to furrow her brow. "Mickey Dann," she said. "As I live and breathe."

"How are you doing?"

"Not well when I meet up with one of the worst math students I ever had."

"I tried," Mickey said sheepishly, silently noting that encounters like this one were among the drawbacks of living in a small town.

"You know, Mickey, I don't think you did. That was the problem. Whatever happened to you, anyway?"

Mickey showed her his badge. "I was in Toronto for a while, now I'm back here with the Halton force."

"You're a police officer?" Mrs. McQueen sounded surprised.

"I'm afraid so."

"I hope you don't have to add two and two."

"Not today," Mickey replied. "I'm looking for one of your guests. A man named Adam Machota."

"You're in luck," Mrs. McQueen said.

"Am I?"

"He's coming along right now."

Mickey saw a tall, dark-haired man walking toward him. Catlike movements, Mickey thought. A guy who immediately telegraphs that he knows how to take care of himself.

Mickey called, "Sergeant Machota."

Machota slowed his walk. "Yes?"

Mickey flashed his identification. "I'm Sergeant Mickey Dann. Halton police. Have you got a moment?"

"I know who you are, sergeant," Machota said.

"Yeah? How would you know that?" Mickey was aware of Mrs. McQueen, eavesdropping behind him.

"You're a friend of Jean's."

"Jean?"

"Jean Whitlock. She and I used to work together."

"So I understand."

"The two of us go way back," Machota said. "You probably heard that I saved her life."

"That's what I'd like to talk to you about," Mickey said.

"Lucky I happened along when I did."

"Why don't we step outside?" To get away from his old math teacher's prying ears, Mickey thought.

"Sure, I was just on my way out anyway."

They went into the parking lot. Machota had his key fob in his hand. "I hope this isn't going to take too long."

"A couple of questions, that's all," Mickey said. "You say you happened to be driving past the house?"

"That's right."

"Quite a coincidence."

"Yeah, I guess you could say that," Machota said. "The good thing is, Jean is alive and that's what counts. Right?"

"Sure," Mickey said. "Mind if ask what you're doing in town?"

"I'm on a leave of absence from the Force. I'll be honest with you, sergeant." Machota flashed a smile to go along with his declaration of honesty. "The stress of an Afghanistan assignment kind of got to me. When we were together in Kandahar, Jean always raved about her hometown. I thought I'd come and see for myself and at the same time visit her."

"A visit with Jean?"

"That's correct. She's been through a lot—we both experienced things together over there. She went through a rocky period. I wanted to make sure she's all right."

"Now you have the added bonus of saving her from a fiery death," Mickey said.

"You make it sound as though I've done something wrong."

"Have you?"

"Saving the life of a colleague? I don't think so, do you?"

"Providing that's what it is."

"Why would it be anything else?"

"The fire is being investigated as arson."

"You think it is arson?"

"It's not up to me. It's what the fire marshal thinks, and right now he's thinking someone started the fire."

"You don't suspect, Jean, do you?" Machota sounded concerned.

"Why would Jean burn down her own house?"

"I guess I'm not surprised that it could be arson," Machota said.

"Oh? What makes you not surprised?"

"Experience, I suppose."

"You have a lot of experience with arson, do you?"

"I don't know that I'd say a lot."

"What were you doing there?"

"What was I doing where?"

"Come on, help me out here," Mickey said. "Why would you be at Jean's house at that time of the morning?"

"Like I told you, I just happened to be driving past."

"It was one-thirty. What were you doing out at that hour?"

"What difference does it make? What matters is that I was there to help."

"Do you mind answering the question?"

Machota grinned, less a reassurance of honesty this time. He looked Mickey up and down, as if seeing him in a different light. "Why do I suspect you have a whole lot more interest in this than the usual police investigation."

"Answer the question," Mickey growled. "What were you doing driving around Milton at one-thirty in the morning?"

"Maybe I don't want to answer any more questions," Machota said. "Maybe this has gone far enough.

I've tried to be co-operative with you. But I detect a note of malice in your questioning."

"Here's the thing, Sergeant Machota," Mickey said, his voice hardening. "I want you to do something for me."

"And what would that be, Sergeant Dann?"

"I want you to stay away from Jean Whitlock while you're in town. Is that clear?"

"This sounds more and more as though I'm being threatened," Machota said.

"You should know that as far as I'm concerned you are no hero, pal. You are a suspect in an arson investigation."

"That's ridiculous," Machota said.

Mickey jabbed a finger. "I know about you, Machota."

"Do you?"

"I know that Jean accused you of attempted rape and murder while the two of you were in Afghanistan."

Machota looked unperturbed. "The Force launched an investigation into those accusations and found them to be without merit."

"So, you're denying you tried to rape and then shoot her?"

"Let me put it this way. I've long since forgiven Jean for what happened in Kandahar. We were both under a lot of strain at the time. My feeling is that we have too much in common to allow the past to get in the way of our future together."

"You're kidding," Mickey said in astonishment. "You don't actually think the two of you have a future."

"There are a lot of things you don't know, Sergeant Dann. Things that I'm sure Jean is keeping from you. But that's all right. I understand."

"Stay away from her," Mickey said.

Machota gave him a smirk. "Is that an order?"

"Something like that, yeah," Mickey answered, his voice hard.

Machota just shrugged. "Good to talk to you, sergeant. I'm glad you came over. Now I know who I'm dealing with."

It wasn't really a threat, Mickey thought. But then it was.

22

I talked to him," Mickey said to Jean when he phoned her.

"Okay," Jean said.

"A cool, cold customer, that's for certain," Mickey said. "Nothing seems to faze him."

"That's because he's a psychopath," Jean said.

"He says he's worried about you," Mickey went on.

"Yeah. Right."

"He says you've been through a bad time. He's in town, he says, to make sure you're okay. He doesn't want to jeopardize his relationship with you. The two of you have too much going."

"That's crap," Jean said, her voice tight with emotion. "We have nothing. There is no relationship. There's only this crazy bastard burning down my house."

"I told him to stay away from you."

"It won't do any good," Jean said.

"Maybe not, but at least he's on notice that police are aware of him and are watching his movements."

"Look, I appreciate you doing this, Mickey."

"It's a legitimate part of the arson investigation," Mickey said. "I'll continue to keep an eye on this guy."

"Thanks."

"Can I make a suggestion?"

"Sure."

"Maybe it's a good idea to disappear for a while. Machota can't hang around here too long I wouldn't think. Presumably he has to go back to work."

"I'm not running away from this asshole," Jean said. "I live in Milton. This is where I was born and where I grew up. I'm not hiding. Besides, he'd just follow me."

"I had no idea you were so committed to this town," Mickey said.

"See what Machota does? He even makes me love my hometown."

"Call me if he bothers you again," Mickey said.

"I will, Mickey. And thanks."

———————

After talking to Jean, Mickey left police headquarters, and drove west along Steeles, and then up to the top of the hill where the developer Del Caulder had built his sprawling glass and wood dream house. Mickey never stopped marveling at the sheer, over-the-top luxury of Del's creation; this monument to excess, the showcase loudly announcing to the locals that Del Caulder had a whole lot more money than they did.

Except, Mickey mused wryly, it also served as a reminder that no matter how much money you've got, no matter how big you build your house on the hill, you can still wind up in jail, asshole.

Mickey could only thank his lucky stars, not to mention the vagaries of the Canadian criminal justice system, that he wasn't in jail, too, given his collusion with Del in the past.

He could also thank his lucky stars as the front door opened and Sharma Caulder stood in the entranceway, that Del wasn't around to see what Mickey was doing with his wife. Sharma looked cross as he came in. "I was beginning to think you had stood me up."

"Sorry, I got delayed at the office."

"You are always delayed at the office," Sharma said with a coquettish pout that at once showed her irritation and her willingness to forgive. "I will try to overlook your tardiness in return for a kiss."

"Yes," Mickey said, "I can do that."

She joined in avidly, as she always did, hungry for something, Mickey was never sure what—his flesh, seemingly, but something more, too. Maybe the human interaction she never received from Del, and certainly wasn't getting now that he was in prison.

He thought they might have sex, their usual routine, but no, she had prepared dinner, a pasta dish. In a way he was relieved. Since meeting Reagan, he desired Sharma less. Besides, their affair made him uneasy. The cop who testified against her husband and helped put him away, now sleeping with the wife of the jailed felon. The optics, to say the least, were not good.

But for now, he continued to see Sharma. The little head, as always, taking command over the big head.

They ate the pasta by the floor-to-ceiling windows overlooking the valley now disappearing in deep shadows as night fell.

They ate pretty much in silence—Mickey never quite sure what to say when they weren't in bed—until Sharma said, "I visited Del today."

This was the first time she had mentioned her husband's name, not surprising since he was the guy who had ultimately betrayed him and put him in jail.

"How's he doing?"

"Terrible," Sharma pronounced. "Yesterday he says he saw a man beaten practically to death and the guards did nothing."

"Yeah, I heard they transferred him to the Elgin Middlesex Detention Center near London."

"Detention Center," she said disdainfully. "This is no detention center. It is a hellhole full of killers. The other inmates told him they would slit his throat if he says anything. But who would he talk to? The prison authorities always look the other way. He is beside himself, very fearful that someone is going to kill him."

"I thought you wanted to kill him." Mickey's attempt at a joke.

She wasn't buying. "*I* want to kill him; I don't want anyone else doing it."

"What can I tell you? He's in prison. Prison is a dangerous place."

"You put him there, Mickey." As though he were to blame for her husband's travails; as though he was responsible for Sharma wanting to screw him.

"Yes, I did," was the only way Mickey could think to respond.

"He believes I'm having an affair," Sharma announced.

"What did you tell him?"

"What do you think I told him? I told him he is crazy."

They finished dinner and just when Mickey didn't think they were going to do anything, she led him upstairs into the bedroom.

"I shouldn't be doing this," she said.

"Neither should I," Mickey said, thinking of Reagan.

Sharma undid his belt, unzipped his pants. "I hate you," she said.

"Yes," he said. He kissed her.

"You know that." She sat on the bed and pulled him to her. "What you did to Del ruined my life."

"Yes," Mickey said.

"Hate you, hate you," Sharma repeated softly.

What the hell was he doing? Then Sharma's mouth devoured him, and he stopped thinking about anything.

———————

Adam Machota broke through a thicket of trees to the edge of a drive leading to the sprawling lightbox at the top of the rise. He could see Mickey Dann's car in front.

Machota had parked at the bottom of the hill and then made his way up on foot. He had seen this house while researching Jean's life after she'd left the Force, the home of Del Caulder, the wealthy real estate developer Jean had helped bring down.

Yes, this was the house, he concluded as he moved forward, keeping to the trees edging the drive. He tried to remember the name of Caulder's wife.

Sharma. That was it.

He reached the side of the house and followed the stonework until he reached a wide terrace jutting over the hill. The valley lay in darkness below.

He crouched down and moved around so that he was just below the terrace with a view of the interior—a dimly lit great room. For a time, the room was deserted. But then two figures appeared. Sergeant Mickey Dann of the Halton Police being led along by a small, beautiful woman who looked to be of South Asian origin. Sharma Caulder? Must be, he thought.

She started up a staircase, Mickey following. At the top of the stairs, she opened a door. The two of them disappeared inside.

The door closed.

Machota couldn't help smiling to himself.

Well, he thought. Well, well.

23

When Doris Clapper bought the Whitlock Funeral Home from Jean, she insisted on retaining the name. The Whitlock family had been a fixture in Milton for generations. The Whitlocks had buried grandparents as well as parents and now as the children of those parents aged and began to die, their children took it for granted Whitlocks would ease the tragedy of death. It made little difference that no one named Whitlock was involved any longer in the business. It was still the Whitlock Funeral Home in Milton, the final stop before the deceased were either cremated—more and more popular—or buried.

Thus, no one was surprised when, after police released the body, Mayor Jock Whitlock moved his wife to the family funeral home. A trifle more surprising, everyone in town agreed, was Jock's decision to place his wife in a casket. A closed casket, granted, but a casket, nonetheless.

The thought around town was that if Jock had killed his wife, and there was speculation that he had, then cremation would have been the fastest and most effective way of destroying any evidence. What was it the police were always looking for? DNA? That was it. Wouldn't DNA be destroyed with the burning of the body?

Doris had done a fine job with the arrangements, but even so the crowd that turned up on a sunny autumn afternoon overwhelmed her best efforts, filling the main reception room, spilling into the hallway.

Jock, again accompanied by his assistant, Grace, and his lawyer, Eddie Fitzgerald, was among the last of the mourners to arrive. He seated himself in the front row facing Desiree's casket—one of the most expensive the funeral home offered—topped with and surrounded by floral arrangements. A glamor shot of Desiree, smiling in happier days, was mounted on an easel next to the casket.

Members of the town council sat behind the mayor, and behind them, Halton dignitaries, members from both the provincial legislature and the federal government. Everyone took turns approaching Jock to offer whispered condolences. Jock stoic, hugged bodies and shook hands, offering a wan smile suggesting strength and determination in the face of tragedy.

Sharma Caulder made her entrance, dazzling in a short black dress, hair swirling luxuriously around a perfectly made-up face, down which tears streamed. She threw herself against the mayor and the tears reached flood proportions. When she finally left Jock, she caught Jean's eye, and instantly snapped her head away, her full mouth tightening in a grimace of disdain. Jean could hardly blame her since she had played a big part putting Del Caulder in jail.

Jean watched her go to an aisle seat not far from where Mickey Dann sat with Glen Petrusiak. By the time she sat down, Sharma had found a handkerchief and was using it to carefully dab at her eyes while simultaneously, Jean couldn't help noticing, casting glances in Mickey's direction.

What was all that about? Or was she imagining things?

The service was presided over by the Reverend Martin James, the pastor at Knox Presbyterian Church. Jean couldn't imagine there was a religious bone in Desiree's body; certainly, there wasn't one in Jock's. Nonetheless, the Rev. James proceeded to lead everyone in prayer.

To his credit the reverend restrained himself from declarations that Desiree was in a better place with the Lord Jesus, and all the other homilies Jean had been forced to listen to over and over again growing up in a small-town funeral home where families wanted the comfort of knowing their deceased loved ones had entered the Kingdom of Heaven.

There was no heaven, Jean had long since decided. Only the hell of living on earth.

Prayers were followed by a hymn—"All Things Bright and Beautiful"—and then speeches. Of course, speeches. Jean reminded herself to leave word that there were to be no speeches at her funeral. But then who was there to speak?

The local Liberal member of parliament spoke as did the member of the provincial legislature, neither of whom seemed to know Desiree, thus delivering pro forma words about how wonderful she was, how she would be missed, how much help she had been to Mayor Jock, even though Jean could not imagine she had been any help at all.

Sharma came next, the taps on full blast for a heart-felt address in a shaky voice, declaring Desiree her best friend in the world. "We were both married to power-ful men," Sharma announced. "We both understood that for all the privileges those men provided us, there was a price to be paid. We talked a lot together, kept each other's secrets together, and, when it was neces-sary, cried together. I will miss her so much."

And then she dissolved into another flood of tears, rushing from the podium. She had not once referred to Desiree's husband.

The service lasted an hour. No one mentioned De-siree's murder. Throughout, Jock sat stoically. He nev-er spoke. When it was over, in the midst of Reverend James's invocation, he got up and quickly left.

As everyone filed out, Jean watched Sharma, who kept glancing at Mickey.

24

For the first time since Jean could remember, Jock didn't want to meet in front of City Hall. Instead, he directed her out to Derry Road where he was building a new house on the land where his old place had stood before fire destroyed it. The skeletal beginnings of what would be a massive two-story edifice rose against a looming escarpment radiant with color now that the leaves had finally turned.

As she parked in the muddy drive, Jean saw him come into view, unaccustomedly in jeans and a windbreaker with a cap pulled down over his eyes; not the smoothly polished mayor today, rather, the rough working man at home on a construction site.

"You look like you're ready to pick up a hammer and go to work," Jean said as she approached him.

"Except I wouldn't know which end of the hammer to use," Jock said.

"A reminder," Jean said. "that appearances are usually deceiving."

"I'm afraid I don't have a tuna sandwich for you today," Jock said.

"I don't like tuna anymore, remember?" Jean said.

"That's right, I forgot. I must be getting old. I keep remembering things the way they used to be."

"Things were never the way they used to be," Jean said.

"We haven't had a chance to talk since the fire," Jock said.

"You've had your own problems," Jean said.

"Still, I should have called."

"There's not much to say," Jean said. "The house is gone. Life's a mess."

"It sure as hell is," Jock agreed.

He turned and nodded toward the skeleton that eventually would become a house. "This was supposed to make amends to Desiree for my various transgressions."

"Like burning down your previous house," Jean said.

"That was an accident," Jock maintained. "Your place, I hear the police think it's arson."

"What's up, Jock? A little nostalgia or is there a real reason why you wanted to see me?"

"I wanted to apologize for the way I carried on the other day. I was upset, obviously. I'd just discovered my wife had been murdered—in Acton, for God's sake. I mean who the hell gets murdered in Acton?"

"You don't have to apologize to me, Jock."

"I didn't kill my wife." Jock looked directly at his niece when he said this.

"Okay," Jean said carefully.

"But the police think I did."

"You know as well as I do that the husband is always a suspect."

"What do you think?"

"I don't think showing up at the murder scene with Eddie Fitzpatrick, was a good idea."

"That makes me a killer?"

"It makes you suspicious. That and the fact no one could find you for at least an hour after the body was discovered."

"I need your help, Jean."

"You keep saying that, Jock, and I keep saying I can't help you. Not with this."

"The police don't have my best interests at heart. You do."

"Do I? I'm not so sure about that."

"I'm your uncle for Christ's sake," Jock flared. "This is blood. You grew up sitting on my lap."

"The evening I found Desiree's body, where were you, Jock?"

"I wasn't in Acton killing her if that's what you're getting at."

"Where were you?"

"Right now, that doesn't make any difference," he said.

"Is that what you told the police?"

"So far I haven't told the police anything."

"You're not talking to the police?"

"On the advice of my attorney."

"That can't go on for long."

"That's why I need your help, Jean. I need you to find the people who were attempting to blackmail Desiree."

"Because?"

"Because I believe the person or persons behind the blackmail may have murdered Desiree."

"The police are equipped to look into this sort of thing. I'm not. You should let the them handle it."

"I don't trust the police. I don't trust this Glen Petrusiak. At least I can trust you. I'm not sure about anyone else."

"The question is, Jock, can I trust you?"

He looked at her with something like surprise. "When have I ever let you down?"

"Don't get me started."

"I love you, Jean. I would never do anything to hurt you." He made it sound as though he'd rehearsed that speech in case he had to use it when they met.

"I don't need you to love me. I need you to be honest. Tell me where you were at the time Desiree was murdered."

He swallowed a couple of times, but his eyes held hers, unblinking. "She mentioned someone named Ryan."

"What do you mean?"

"I heard her talking on the phone a couple of weeks ago. Very intense. She called the person she was talking to, Ryan. Maybe Ryan was trying to extort money from her. Maybe that's a starting point."

"It's not much to go on," Jean said.

"Please," Jock said. "Please do this for me, Jean. Find something that proves my innocence—before I'm arrested for something I didn't do."

———

The part she hadn't told Jock, the part she hadn't told anyone, the part that allowed her to convince herself to help her uncle was Adam Machota showing up at the Bethel Church in Acton moments after she discovered Desiree's body.

Was he simply following her and happened upon the scene? Or was there something more? Could the man who burned down her house have played a role in Desiree's murder?

She thought of this driving on Steeles Avenue as it looped to the top the hill where Del Caulder's glass palace glinted in sunlight poking intermittently through scuttling clouds. Del's monument to himself, to the power of moving earth and gobbling up farmland for more condo developments, she mused as she got to the front gate.

But that had changed, hadn't it? Sharma Caulder was now in charge. She held the power previously wielded by her husband. The question everyone in town quietly asked was, how would she use it?

This was the Sharma who hated Jean's guts. The Sharma who blamed Jean for her husband's incarceration. The Sharma who apparently had yet to reach the point where she might concede that Del's own actions might have something to do with his imprisonment.

The Sharma who probably would refuse to talk to her.

Jean reached out the window to press the intercom next to the gate. A disembodied voice, lost in a rain of static, erupted from the intercom's speaker.

"It's Jean Whitlock. I'm here to see Sharma."

Nothing for a time and then finally a whirring sound as the gates opened and she drove through. Sharma in jeans and a white blouse was waiting for her at the door. She did not look happy.

"I don't want you in my house," Sharma said defiantly.

"That's fine, but I need to talk to you."

"We can talk out here." Sharma folded her arms and spread her legs, prepared to block the way should Jean make a break for the house. "What's this about?" she demanded.

"I need to talk to you about Desiree," Jean said.

"What's there to talk about?"

"Someone killed her, I'd like to know who did it."

"Why should you care?" Sharma asked sullenly.

"Desiree reached out to me for help. I got there too late. I found her in her car with her throat cut. I owe it to her to try to figure out who would do this and why. I didn't know the two of you were close until I heard you speak at the funeral."

"No one knew," Sharma said. "I mean, people knew we were acquaintances, but we were much closer than that. And why wouldn't we be? We were both married to a couple of shits, weren't we? One of those shits is in jail. The other shit should be."

"Is that how Desiree thought of Jock? A shit?"

"It came and went depending on what new horror Jock unleashed on her. But generally, yeah, that's how we both felt."

"Is that why she was having an affair?"

"Did she tell you that?"

Jean nodded. "That's why someone was attempting to blackmail her."

"Blackmail?" Sharma looked genuinely surprised. "She said she was being blackmailed?"

"She didn't say anything to you?"

Sharma shook her head. "No. Nothing."

"But you knew she was having an affair."

"Not for sure," Sharma said. "But the way she was talking, I suspected something was going on."

"The name Ryan. Does that mean anything?"

Sharma nodded. "Yes, she talked about Ryan. As a friend. But Ryan wouldn't kill her, if that's what you're getting at."

"Why not? Why wouldn't Ryan do it?"

"Because," Sharma said, "Ryan is a woman."

"Do you know where I can find her?"

"Desiree never said much about her. Ryan was a friend, that's all. I'm not sure there was much more to it than that."

25

"What's she saying, that my wife was a lesbian?" Jock asked in a lifeless voice after Jean reported what Sharma had told her.

They were having dinner at the Thai House. Jock had spent the first twenty minutes shaking hands and nodding solemnly as well-wishers stopped by to express sympathy.

"Sharma's claiming Ryan is a woman, that's all," Jean countered. "A friend."

"That would make her a lesbian, wouldn't it?" Jock sounded angry.

"It's a name, that's all," Jean said. "It doesn't make Desiree anything."

Jock sat back, shaking his head. "Jesus Christ."

"Sharma believes that because Ryan is a woman, she couldn't have killed Desiree."

"What do you think?"

"First of all, we don't know for sure what or who Ryan is, and secondly, at this point you can't rule out anyone, male or female, as a possible suspect."

Jock poured his third glass of red wine, emptying the bottle he had ordered when he sat down. "You should go easy," Jean said.

"Yeah, well, I should do a lot of things," Jock said. He drank deeply from the glass.

"Jock, I know this is a difficult time." Jean said. "But you need to keep it together."

Jock snorted out what passed for a laugh. "Jesus Christ, wasn't it only yesterday I was giving *you* advice?"

"You're staying in a rented house for the moment, are you not?" Jean asked.

"That's right."

"Have the police searched it?"

Jock shook his head. "Eddie Fitzgerald told them they needed a warrant."

"So, they haven't been around," Jean said.

"Not yet," Jock said.

"I'm surprised," Jean said. "This *is* a murder investigation."

"I think maybe Eddie's got them spooked."

"I'd like to take look in the house before they get in there," Jean said.

"I've already gone through the place, there's nothing."

"Let me take a look."

Jock smirked. "Trained professional, huh?"

"Something like that," Jean agreed.

"Let me think about it."

Jean gave him a surprised look. In return, Jock made a face. "I'm just not ready for this right now."

"You're making it hard for me to help you."

Jock looked at his watch. "I'd better get going. There's a council meeting first thing tomorrow, and I have to get ready for it."

———

Jean tried to convince herself that there was nothing suspicious about Jock's refusal to allow her into his house.

She tried, but she couldn't quite do it.

Instead, she began to consider what he might be hiding. Whatever it was—if it was anything—it was not evidence that would exonerate him. For the first time, she allowed herself to address the notion that Jock might actually have killed his wife.

But Jock was too cool a customer for something that needed furious, jealous passion. It would require a man who could lose control in a split second and do the unthinkable to a woman he supposedly loved.

Jock was not that man.

Or was he?

With her suspicions aroused, it wasn't much of a stretch, knowing Jock was in a town council meeting, to drive to his house the next morning.

Have a quick look, see for herself what she might be getting into with Jock. As though she should be getting involved with anything to do with her uncle at this point.

Still, he was her uncle. So, a look.

The house Jock and Desiree had rented while their new place was under construction occupied a corner lot in one of the bland developments that had turned Milton into the fastest-growing town in Canada. A big, brick affair, it stood like a fort guarding the street—or holding onto secrets, Jean thought as she parked.

In the gray afternoon, with the temperature dropping and the wind rising, the street stood deserted—

save for the mayor's niece about to break and enter. Well, not exactly, since she was able find the spare key under the mat at the back door—exactly where Desiree had left it for the cleaning woman. Jean unlocked the door and stepped into a sparkling kitchen, the bare granite counters camera-ready for an HGTV episode featuring a couple deciding to rent a space that provided no sign whatsoever of actual habitation.

The living room looked as pristine and untouched as the kitchen. A Robert Bateman print of a majestic bison hung over the fireplace, although Jean would have bet money neither Desiree nor Jock had anything to do with setting it there.

The massive bed in the master bedroom had not been made, the only sign Jean so far had encountered that Jock actually lived here. Off the bedroom was a huge walk-in closet. Very little sign of Jock here, either; most of the space was taken up with Desiree's clothes. The lower shelves displayed dozens of designer shoes. Christian Louboutin would be proud. Jean, on the other hand, couldn't help but be a little envious.

She was still admiring Desiree's vast array of shoes when she heard a noise.

Running water. A shower.

Someone else was in the house.

26

Jean stepped into the hallway to peer over the banister. The sound of the water came from below.

Someone else was definitely in the house.

Presently, she heard footsteps in the lower hall. The aroma of brewing coffee filled the air.

Jean crept down the stairs to the ground floor. The rush of the shower mixed with the gurgle of percolating coffee. She stood listening, facing the entrance hall. A woman appeared out of the kitchen. She held a coffee mug. Jean focused on the words MR. MAYOR stenciled on its side.

Grace Travis in a white terrycloth robe, her damp gray hair swept back from her forehead, stood open-mouthed, staring at Jean. In a weak voice, she said, "Jean. What are you doing here?"

Jean answered, "I might ask you the same thing, Grace."

"I've got a shower running," Grace said, as if it were the most natural thing in the world to be showering at the mayor's house. She added, "I'd better turn it off."

"Yes," Jean said.

"There's coffee in the kitchen," Grace said, and then disappeared down the stairs.

Jean entered the kitchen. The coffee maker was on the counter. She found a cup in the cupboard.

Grace came in as Jean poured coffee. She was still in her robe. She said, "There's milk in the refrigerator."

"You seem to know your way around here," Jean said, going to the refrigerator.

"Well, I know where the milk is," Grace said.

Jean found a carton of two-percent milk on a lower shelf. She poured some into her cup. "How long has this been going on?" she asked.

"How long has what been going on?"

"You and the mayor."

Grace's mouth tightened. "You still haven't told me what you're doing here."

"I'm supposed to be helping Jock prove he didn't kill his wife. Now I know why he didn't want me snooping around his house."

"No, I don't suppose he did."

"Answer the question, Grace. How long has this been going on between the two of you."

"I'm not going to lie to you, Jean. Years, I suppose, when I think about it. Years since I made the mistake of falling in love with your uncle."

"Even though he married Desiree?"

The tightening of Grace's mouth became more pronounced. "We were going to marry after he divorced his first wife. Then he met Desiree…" Her voice trailed off.

"And suddenly you weren't going to marry."

Grace shrugged. "I couldn't compete with her glamor, I suppose."

"But you didn't leave your job with him."

"He insisted he wanted me to stay, and I chose to stay. And whatever there was between us, it was always a secret. No one else knew."

"Except, here you are in the mayor's house, making yourself at home, taking a shower, having morning coffee in one of Desiree's housecoats."

Grace looked offended. "This is *my* housecoat," she said insistently. "I don't touch any of her things. I don't go upstairs. I refuse to go up there. That's their space. Their life."

"A life that has ended."

Grace dropped her eyes. "Very sad," she said. "A tragedy."

"The police suspect Jock murdered Desiree."

"Yes," she said quietly. "I'm aware of that."

"You're not helping dissuade them from their suspicions."

Grace's eyes flashed angrily. "What do you mean by that?"

"Someone might jump to the conclusion that Jock killed his wife so that he could be with his longtime, loyal assistant."

Grace's mouth made that tightening movement again. "Your uncle's a bugger," she said. "Nobody knows that better than me. Impossible to live with. Things were not good between him and Desiree."

"You knew that?"

"Of course, I knew. What do you think brought us back together? He believed she was having an affair."

"What did you think?"

"I mean, I always thought Desiree was an unreliable tramp, but all I knew was what Jock told me."

"So, no shortage of reasons for Jock to kill his wife."

"Is that what you believe, Jean?"

"What do you believe?"

"Like I said. He's a bugger. But he's not a killer."

"It would go a long way toward proving his innocence if it turns out he was with you on the day Desiree was murdered."

Grace's mouth tightened again. "That could be a problem," she said.

"How is that?"

"We weren't together that day. He wasn't even in the office."

"Do you know where he was?"

Grace shook her head. "I have no idea."

27

"I have had to deal with many policemen, but no one from the Mounted Police," Sharma Caulder stated. "Don't you wear like a red tunic or something?"

"I'm sorry?" queried Adam Machota.

"You understand? The Mounties. Where I grew up in Pakistan, we believed all the Mounted Police wore red and those hats with the funny, round brims."

"Only on ceremonial occasions nowadays," Machota said, smiling. "Serving members wear brown uniforms to perform their day-to-day duties."

Sharma inspected his ID some more and then studied him closely, her darting eyes full of suspicion. "But you're not even wearing a uniform. Why is that?"

"As I explained, I'm a sergeant with the Force, assigned to plainclothes duties."

"I do not like policemen."

"I understand that," Machota said. "You're not in trouble, Mrs. Caulder. It won't take long. Just a few minutes."

She handed him back his ID, less apprehensive than she was when he first appeared at her door. "All right, you may come in, but just for a few minutes."

"That's very kind of you," Machota said, stepping inside.

Sharma allowed herself to concede that even without the uniform this Sergeant Machota was handsome, nicely proportioned in his blue suit, a pleasant odor about him. Even though she was sick and tired of policemen, Mickey Dann included—definitely Mickey Dann—she decided that it wouldn't hurt to hear this one out.

Besides, what else did she have to do with herself these days? Screw cops. Hate cops. Screw them again. Hate them even more.

Sharma led him into the living room with its spectacular view of the vibrant landscape below the escarpment, Lake Ontario just visible in the hazy distance. Machota looked duly impressed. "You have a lovely home, Mrs. Caulder."

"Yes, thank you," Sharma said. "The authorities have repeatedly tried to take it away, but so far they have failed. I hope you are not here to try again."

"Not at all."

"Sit down, please. Can I get you something?"

"I'm fine for the moment, thanks," Machota said, seating himself on one of the sofas.

She sat across from him, noticing that he noticed the way she crossed her legs. She thought of Mickey Dann and then thought, no, she had had enough of cops. She told herself to behave, focusing as he produced notebook and pen.

"First of all, I should say that what I'm about to discuss with you is highly confidential, Mrs. Caulder."

"Yes, all right." Sharma gave him a mystified look.

"It should not go beyond the confines of this room. Do you understand?"

More mystified than ever she said, "Yes."

"Good. I appreciate your cooperation." Machota paused, and then continued in a more formal voice: "The Force has mounted a far-reaching investigation in connection with our American law enforcement partners. The investigation concerns a crime syndicate operating on both sides of the border with tentacles reaching deep into Mexico, and the drug cartels in that country.

"This syndicate does a huge business—billions, we estimate—illegally importing opioids such as OxyContin, Fentanyl, and Vicodin from Mexico, through the United States and then into this country via Niagara Falls. Until now these people have acted with what amounts to impunity, due largely to the payoffs they make to corrupt local police officials. I've been tasked to investigate police corruption in the Halton region. As a result of our inquiries, we now have reason to believe that members of the Halton police are involved in this trafficking."

Sharma listened, her face revealing degrees of puzzlement. She said, "I'm sorry to hear this. I am certainly against drugs, but I don't see how this has anything to do with me."

"One of the Halton police officers we're investigating is a detective named Mickey Dann. You know this man."

It was not a question. Sharma felt her stomach drop. "I know that he is one of the people responsible for putting my husband in prison," she said.

"Here's the thing, Mrs. Caulder," Machota said. "In the course of looking into Dann's activities, we have concluded he concocted much of the evidence that led to your husband's conviction."

The puzzlement was replaced by surprise. "I don't understand what you're saying. Sergeant Dann made things up that were then used to convict my husband?"

"We believe so, yes."

"If that's correct, what would it mean?"

"It could lead to the charges against your husband being thrown out and his release from prison."

"My God," Sharma said, hardly able to believe what she was hearing.

"However, bringing Dann to justice is not going to be easy. He is clever and resourceful. We are going to need all the help we can get in order to convict this person. That's where you come in, Mrs. Caulder."

"Me?" Sharma gave Machota a quizzical look. "How could I possibly help?"

"Look, Mrs. Caulder, we're both adults, so I don't need to dress this up. We've been following Dann for some time. We know the two of you have been seeing each other."

Sharma looked momentarily stricken before pulling herself together. She announced, "That's not true."

"I don't care who you do or do not associate with, it's none of my concern. But I do care about seeing justice done, and you can help us ensure that it is. Would you like to know what we have concluded?"

"All right," Sharma said, not certain what to expect.

"We have concluded that the reason Detective Mann falsified the evidence that put your husband in prison was so he could get to you."

Sharma blinked in astonishment. "You really think this is true?"

"It's hard to reach any other conclusion."

"I have to be honest with you," Sharma said.

"I appreciate that," Machota said.

"It will sound strange to you."

"That's all right."

"I sleep with him."

"Yes."

"Because I hate him."

"Then help us get him," Machota said.

28

The receptionist at the GoodLife gym facility happily provided Jean with a guest pass.

For the next hour she worked out on a cross-trainer and then used the weight machines. Other than a good workout, she was not certain what she was looking for beyond the fact that Desiree had been spending a lot of time here recently.

She was doing reps with a pair of ten-pound hand weights in front of a wall mirror, lamenting the sorry state of her body when she was approached by a young man with a shaved head and a body that actually looked as though it belonged in a gym. "That's great for your shoulders," the young man offered.

"It is?" Jean replied.

"Really well-toned shoulders can look very attractive," the young man continued.

"Shoulders are the least of my problems," Jean said.

She put the weights down and the young man held out of his hand. "My name's Cameron. I'm one of the personal trainers here. I understand you're interested in joining."

"Looking to get back into shape, for sure," Jean said.

"You look good—"

"For a woman my age?" Jean interjected.

Cameron gave her an embarrassed smile that made him look all the more boyish. "That's not what I was going to say," he said.

"I'm sure," Jean said.

"Tell you what. I've got lots of information we hand out to prospective guests. Why don't I put together a package that you can look over and decide on next steps?"

"Fair enough," Jean said.

Cameron said he would be right back. She wandered over to a wall displaying photographs of the gym's personal trainers. Bright young faces, eager to whip a client into shape to "fulfill your goals." What were her goals? Jean wondered. She had no idea. Work out and eat right? Sure, why not?

Cameron grinned at her from his photo. He had graduated with a degree in physical education from a community college she had never heard of. Beside Cameron was a photo of a pretty young woman named Tara Ryan. A certified level-four personal trainer, according to the bio below the photo. Whatever that was.

Ryan?

Or was it just a coincidence? Unlike the others, Tara Ryan did not smile quite so brightly; more of a pout, Jean thought. A look that said, Come and get me; I'm not coming to you.

Or was she imagining things?

"Here we go." Jean swung around to see Cameron with a white folder that he pushed into her hands. "This should tell you all you need to know."

"I didn't realize Tara Ryan worked here," Jean said.

"You know Ryan?"

"Is that what everyone calls her?"

"No one calls her Tara," Cameron said.

"A friend of mine says she's a great trainer."

Cameron's face darkened, losing some of its boyishness sensing a potential client slipping away. "She's very good," he said without enthusiasm.

"Could I book a session with her?"

"She's here in an hour or so, and I don't think she's got anything scheduled."

"I'd like to work with her if that's okay with you," Jean said.

"Sure, fine." Cameron managed to reignite his smile as he said, "They'll take care of you at the desk."

She looked at the photo again.

Ryan.

————

Tara Ryan—"nobody calls her Tara"—came in three-quarters of an hour later. Tall, lithe, with long, golden hair done in a ponytail, Ryan could serve as the poster child for healthy lifestyle choices. She spoke briefly to Cameron, a conversation punctuated by a quick glance or two in Jean's direction.

Then she sauntered over. "Hi, I'm Ryan," she said.

Jean introduced herself and they shook hands. "How's your day so far?" Ryan inquired. What was it about the serving millennials who always wanted to know what kind of day you were having, Jean wondered. They all seemed to be programmed with the same question.

"So far, my day is fine," Jean answered. "How is your day, Ryan?"

"Great." Quick smile. "I just finished a 10-k. run, so I'm pumped and ready."

For what? Jean wondered. Aloud she said, "Good for you."

"Hey, Jean. I'm looking forward to a great relationship with you. I understand you asked for me specifically."

"I've heard great things about you," Jean said.

"It's so gratifying to hear that," Ryan said. "So, let's look at where you are right now and what your goals are."

"Does everyone have to have goals?" Jean asked.

Ryan managed a smile. "No, of course not. But if you have a place where you want to get to, that's where I can be really, really helpful. I want to be there so that you can reach your full potential."

"I wonder what my full potential looks like."

Ryan flashed another smile. "That's the journey you and I take together. Along the way, I can also help you with lifestyle, nutrition, stress management."

"I feel like a better human being already," Jean said.

"Great," Ryan said brightly. "We're already making progress. Let's take a look at a few machines so I can see where you are now in terms of a workout."

"We can do that," Jean said. "But first of all, I'd like to know a little more about you. Have you been doing this for long?"

"A few years now," Ryan said, noncommittally.

"You're very young to be changing people's lives."

"Is there an age when you're supposed to start?"

"Apparently not," Jean answered. "Are you from around here?"

"Out west, originally."

"Where out west?"

"I was born in Oakville"

"How did you end up in Milton?"

The smile wasn't so much flashed this time as forced. "Hey, we're getting a bit turned around here, Jean. I'm supposed to be asking you questions. Finding out what makes you tick."

"I'm curious about a person who's going to transform me into a better human being, that's all."

"A *healthier* human," she amended, trying to keep it light, but tensing.

"A mutual friend recommended you," Jean said.

"That's good to know," Ryan said and then fell silent. Jean waited for her to ask who had made the recommendation. She didn't.

Finally, Jean said, "Don't you want to know who the friend is?"

"Sure, if you want to tell me."

"Desiree Whitlock. She's a huge fan."

"That's very kind of her." Her voice had become flat, lifeless.

"You know who I'm talking about?"

"Desiree is a client."

"Do you know what's happened to her?"

Ryan's face had become a blank landscape. "What's this about?"

"You know Desiree is dead?"

"You know what? You might be better off with one of our other trainers," Ryan said, her voice tight.

"No, you're the one I want," Jean said.

There was no more smiling. "I meet with prospective clients so I can get a feel for them. This only works if there is some sort of chemistry with the client. I'm not feeling any chemistry with you."

"I'm sorry to hear that, Ryan. You know that Desiree was murdered?"

Ryan looked momentarily stricken before she said, "Fuck off," and then strode off.

The next thing, Cameron was in Jean's face. He no longer looked so boyish. "I don't think it's going to work for you at this gym," he said.

"No? Funny, I was just beginning to feel at home here."

"I think you'd better leave," Cameron said.

"Careful, Cameron," Jean said in a warning voice. "You don't want to be on my bad side, believe me."

Cameron's face darkened more, and he looked even less boyish. He made an ugly noise before walking away.

29

Tara Ryan came out of the gym an hour later. She was on her cellphone as she waited beneath the portico. Presently, Cameron came out and joined her. She pocketed her cellphone. He put his arm around her, kissed her briefly, then the two of them went over to where a Jeep Cherokee was parked and climbed in. Cameron was behind the wheel, Ryan back on her cellphone as the Jeep started out of the parking lot. When the Jeep reached Steeles Avenue, it turned right.

Jean followed the Jeep along Steeles to a roundabout where it turned south onto Tremaine Road. By the time the Jeep swung onto Derry Road, traffic had thinned considerably. Jean stayed well back as the road twisted past Rattle Snake Point. Cameron turned onto Guelph Line as it swooped into a valley towards Lowville.

Just past the Lowville Bistro, the Jeep turned sharply right into a parking area. Ryan and Cameron had reached the Lowville Park.

Jean pulled into one of the parking spaces at the bistro and got out in time to see Ryan emerge from the Jeep while Cameron remained inside. Jean watched as the young woman, ponytail bobbing, jogged toward the pathway beside Bronte Creek. Jean got back into her vehicle and drove across to park at the back of the lot well away from the Jeep.

From this vantage point, Jean watched Ryan follow the pathway to a bridge. She crossed to where pleasantly shaded picnic tables were stationed along the creek. Jean could see Ryan reach one of the tables where a man, talking on his cellphone, was seated.

Jean got out of her car and stood watching as Ryan threw her arms around the man rising awkwardly to his feet.

The man was Milton Mayor Jock Whitlock.

Jean turned her attention to the Jeep. Cameron was outside holding what looked like a video camera with a long lens.

Back at the picnic table, Ryan continued kissing Jock. Finally, she pulled away and sat at the table. Jock's shoulders slumped and then he rallied and joined her.

Jean could see them lean into each other, bodies tensed. Cameron, meanwhile, continued aiming his video camera in their direction.

Jean went back to her van, opened the glove box and pulled out the baton she kept there. With the baton in hand, she strode to the Jeep.

Cameron's back was to her as she made the smooth hand motion that snapped the baton out to its full length. He heard the sound and turned as Jean smashed the camera, knocking it out of his hand. It shattered against the pavement.

Cameron cried out in alarm. Jean swung the baton against the side of his head. He grunted and fell back against the Jeep. Jean shoved the baton against his throat long enough to fish the keys out of his jeans pocket and then his cellphone. She got the driver's-side door open and thrust Cameron, now bleeding from a gash in his head, into the cab. She climbed in after him, pushing him to the passenger side, and slamming the door shut. She glanced over to where Ryan was sitting with Jock. Neither of them had noticed anything.

Meanwhile, Cameron, against the passenger-side door, was groaning and holding his bleeding head. Blood trickled through his fingers. "What the—"

"Shut up, Cameron," she snapped. "I'm a cop. Now shut up and just answer some questions. Understand?"

Cameron slowly nodded.

"You were meeting Desiree in Acton to extort money from her, right?"

When Cameron didn't say anything, Jean grabbed him by the T-shirt front and slammed him against the side widow. "Cameron, answer me."

"Yes. Jesus. But she was dead when I got there."

"Don't tell me you're stupid enough to try the same thing with Jock."

"It's Ryan. She's on my ass to do this shit. Thinks she's some badass criminal or something."

Jean tossed the cellphone into his lap. "Here's what you do. You call Ryan. You tell her she has to come back to the Jeep. Now. Do that. You understand?"

It took a moment, but Cameron finally acknowledged her demand with another nod. Jean pushed the cellphone into his hand and watched while he poked out a number. When Ryan came on the line, Jean could hear her say, "Yes?"

"Get out of there. Now," Cameron mumbled.

"What?"

"Just do it," Cameron said.

He closed the phone and dropped it to his lap. "My goddamn head hurts," he complained.

"Next thing, Cameron, and listen carefully. When Ryan gets back, the two of you drive off. You go to the police and tell them what you told me. I'll give you twenty-four hours to do it. If you don't, I'll call them myself and it will be that much worse for you. Do you understand what I'm saying?"

"Yeah, okay," Cameron said between gritted teeth.

Jean tossed him the keys and then opened the door and got out. She stooped to pick up the broken camera. She could see Ryan crossing the bridge. She went back to the van and fumbled with the camera until she found the memory card. By then the Jeep was pulling out of the parking lot. She watched it disappear up the road before turning her attention to Jock. He remained at the picnic table, hunched over, as if in prayer.

Jean crossed the bridge and came along the path to where Jock was seated with his back to her. He didn't see her until she slid onto the seat across from him. He lifted his head and Jean registered, with some satisfaction, his shocked expression.

"Jesus Christ," he said.

"Are you out of your mind?" Jean asked.

"What the hell are you doing here?"

"Wondering how you can be so careless."

"What's that supposed to mean?"

Jean placed the memory card in front of him. "While you were making out with your true love, her boyfriend was in the parking lot with a camera."

Jock stared at the memory card, saying nothing. Then he lifted his head and said, "There must be some mistake."

"God, Jock. Don't start with a lot of lame excuses. They were doing the same thing with Desiree. Ryan and her boyfriend, Cameron, are on their way to the police now to explain what happened."

"You're not going to tell me they murdered Desiree."

"Cameron says she was dead when he got to Acton. For now, I tend to believe him. We'll see what the police think."

Jock looked confused. "I don't understand what's going on. How did you know where to find me?"

"I didn't," Jean said.

"Then how did you get here?"

"What did Ryan tell you?"

"You mean, Tara? She said a woman came to the gym asking all sorts of weird questions. It spooked her."

"I was the woman asking the weird questions," Jean said.

"Why would you be asking Tara anything?"

"Because I was looking for the person who was having an affair with your wife."

"What are you talking about? Tara was not having an affair with my wife."

"She's not now, but she was. Or hasn't she told you?"

Jock blanched. "You must be insane."

"Desiree knew her as Ryan. Tara Ryan. Didn't any of this occur to you?"

"Jesus Christ," Jock said, exhaling loudly. "You're supposed to be helping me."

"I'm trying to. But every time I turn around, there you are getting yourself deeper into trouble."

Jock lowered his head, as though resuming prayer. "Shit," he said quietly.

"Look, if those two idiots do what they're supposed to do, then very soon you're going to have to explain yourself to the police. You may be under arrest; Tara and her boyfriend, Cameron, too."

"Why would I be arrested?"

"Conspiring with your friends Ryan and Cameron to murder your wife might be one of the reasons. You're having an affair with Ryan—or Tara, as you know her. You discover she's also sleeping with your wife. You kill your wife so you can be with Tara."

"Shit," Jock repeated.

"What about Grace?" Jean asked.

"What about her?"

"Does she know about this double and triple life you've been leading?"

"Grace doesn't count in this," Jock said sullenly.

"That's not what she thinks," Jean said.

"How would you know what Grace thinks?"

"Because when I went around to your house, she was in her housecoat about to take a shower."

"Jesus, I told you not to go around there," Jock flared angrily.

"It's probably a good thing I'm not listening to you. For God's sake, Jock, when do you find time to run the town?"

An elderly Asian man, leaning hard on a cane, struggled past, escorted by a young woman who looked as though she could be his daughter. The young woman smiled at Jean. The old man struggled on.

Jock, hands clasped in front of him, once more lowered his head, as if to plead for mercy from a higher being. Jean didn't think it was coming any time soon.

"I don't know what to do," Jock muttered.

"I shouldn't be advising you," Jean said. "You need to get hold of Eddie Fitzpatrick and the two of you should go to the police and tell them what you know."

"I didn't kill my wife." The statement came out with a whole lot less certainty than Jock intended.

"Grace says you weren't with her the day Desiree was killed. Were you with Ryan?"

Jock his head. "No."

"Where were you?"

Jock hesitated before he said, "It doesn't matter."

"It's going to matter to the police."

Instead of answering, Jock looked at his watch. "I'm sorry, I have to go," he announced. "I can't deal with this right now." He started up.

"Jock—"

"I'll be in touch." He was on his feet. "It'll be all right, I know it will."

"No, it won't, Jock. Simply saying it will be all right won't make it so."

Wordlessly, he turned and walked away. She watched him cross the bridge to the parking lot.

30

On a gray, windy autumn day the driving range, closed for the season, stood gloomy and deserted. A wood shed fronted a long platform topped with AstroTurf that looked out on an open field, marked at intervals with white-painted signs, peeling badly, identifying the number of yards the practicing golfer had hit a ball.

Adam Machota sat on a bench at the side of the shed, admiring the autumn colors dotting the distant escarpment, zipping up his windbreaker against the biting wind, regretting he hadn't worn something warmer. He stood, shoving his hands into his pockets. Presently, he heard the sound of a motor and the crunch of gravel. A car had pulled in. The driver extracted herself with difficulty and then started toward the waiting Machota. As he watched her approach Machota thought of the word, lumbering.

"Hello, Adam," Inspector Jill Lowry called.

He couldn't help but notice how out of place she seemed without her Mounted Police uniform. The uniform smoothed her out somewhat, provided an elegance she lacked this afternoon in her wintery padded coat that made her bulky and misshapen. An old woman. Who lived in a shoe? Well, not quite, although Jill Lowry would certainly fit that role.

"Did you have any trouble finding it?" Machota asked.

She shook her head. "You might have found something a little warmer. I'm not getting any younger."

"This way, maybe you'll keep it short," Adam said.

"My goodness, Adam, why are you so impatient with me?"

Machota said nothing.

Jill Lowry's eyes narrowed to inspect him. "Are you all right?"

"Let's sit over here," he said, indicating the bench.

"Yes, that's fine." She headed for the bench, her breathing a little raspy, he thought. With her back to him, she said, "You haven't answered my question."

"It's all good," Machota said.

Inspector Lowry plopped herself down on the bench. Her face was red. "Ah, that's better, she said.

"Why are you so interested in my health?" Machota asked seating himself beside her.

"The most diplomatic answer to that is this: some of our people are worried."

"Some?"

"Put it this way. More people than should be worried are worried."

"Which accounts for you driving down here from Ottawa."

"A chance to see a friend—and a colleague. Ensure that things are working the way they should and address any problems if they're not."

"I don't see any difficulties. But tell me about these unnamed people. What are their concerns?"

"The most pressing concern is that all this is taking too long, that you've embarked on some sort of crazy revenge thingy, and you are out of control."

"Revenge thingy," Adam said with a smirk. "You know, Jill, everyone thinks you're their beloved grand-mother or something. But I know better. I know you for what you are."

"And what would that be, Adam?"

"How about ruthless, conniving bitch."

Instead of becoming angry, as Machota had expected, Jill bestowed one of her gentle smiles, the smile that irritated him no end, the smile that said, 'I am better and wiser than you.'

"Adam, you're not answering. Reassure me that you are in control of the situation here."

"Look, we are baiting a trap, and baiting traps takes time," Machota answered, trying to maintain a reasonable tone. "You say our friend threatens our entire operation. Correct?"

"I say that, yes."

"And I agree with you. So, how do we accomplish our goal? If you get on a plane and fly to Afghanistan, then you are attempting to take him out on his own turf, and believe me, that's not going to work. The best thing then is to lure him onto our turf. Jean is the bait. He will come for her."

"If she calls him," Jill said.

"She will call him," Machota said adamantly. "We just have to keep up the pressure on her. Remove the support systems that could protect her. Then she has no choice but to call him for help."

"This local police detective, Mickey Dann."

"Yes, he's part of her support system. We need him marginalized."

"Another area of concern."

"With Dann out of the way, Jean will be a lot more likely to make the call we want her to make."

Inspector Lowry was silent for a time. She seemed to huddle deeper into her winter coat before she said, "Did I tell you I'm retiring?"

Machota gave her a surprised look. "You know damned well you didn't."

"It hasn't been announced yet, but I'll be gone by the end of the year."

"What's that mean?"

"For one thing I will no longer be able to protect your ass."

"I don't need your protection, Jill."

"Don't you? It seems to me that if I hadn't interceded, made sure that Jean Whitlock was accelerated out of the Force, you might be sitting in a prison cell convicted of attempted rape and murder."

"That's where you're wrong," Machota said insistently. "You did exactly what you were supposed to do, find me innocent of those charges. I didn't do anything to Jean. Anything that went on between us was entirely consensual."

Jill gave him a long look and then said, "I just want you to be careful, Adam. As I've made clear, other people are feeling the same way I do. If this doesn't soon work, then those people will come to the conclusion that your actions are endangering all of us."

"What is that?" Machota demanded. "Is that a threat?"

"There are no threats, Adam. Words of advice, that's all." Jill Lowry shivered. "Now I'm getting a chill." She gave Adam another of her beatific smiles. He wanted to strangle her. "I'd better be getting back to Ottawa. Do you need anything else?"

"Knowing I have your support is enough for me."

She chose not to hear the sarcasm in his voice. "I'm glad you feel that way. Please keep in touch."

"You can depend on it," Machota said.

He watched her trudge back to her car. Fat, malicious cow, he thought. Not to be trusted.

None of them could be trusted. Only Jean. He could trust her. When they were finally together, he would trust her completely.

31

He still makes me do things, you know," Sharma said.

For a moment, Mickey thought she was referring to something sexual. They were lying in bed having just made love.

"He's in jail," Mickey said. "How weird can it get?"

"I'm not talking about that sort of thing," Sharma said.

"What are you talking about?"

"Errands he wants me to run for him."

"You're not involved in any shit, are you?"

"Come with me," Sharma said. She rose from the bed and reached for her robe. "There's something I want to show you."

He pulled on his jeans and followed her out to the garage. She ordered him to move a trestle table away from the wall. "Okay, now what?" Did he sound impatient? Probably. He didn't like where this might be headed, and the faster they got there, the better he could deal with it.

Sharma extracted a screwdriver from a tool box on the table and used it to take out the screws holding a metal panel in the wall. Once the screws were out, she removed the panel to reveal a cavity stuffed with bundles of currency wrapped in plastic.

"What the hell is that?" Mickey demanded. As if he didn't know.

"Money," Sharma said, rising to her feet. "What's it look like?"

"It looks like the trouble you're about to get me into," Mickey said.

"Del's rainy-day fund."

The money the courts didn't get, Mickey thought. Out loud he said, "Sharma, I'm a police officer. I can't be doing this."

"You don't worry about being a police officer when you are fucking me," Sharma shot back.

"This is different."

"You're worrying when there's nothing to worry about," Sharma said insistently.

"What are you supposed to do with this?"

"A friend of Del's. I'm supposed to deliver one hundred and fifty thousand dollars to him. It's a lot of money. I don't want be alone with it. I will feel much better if you are with me."

"Jesus, Sharma, don't do this to me," Mickey said.

"I'm not doing anything except asking you for help."

"Where are you going to make this delivery?"

"Del's friend is in Niagara Falls."

"Niagara Falls," Mickey said in dismay. "You're kidding."

"Quit saying I'm kidding. I'm not kidding. This must be done to protect Del."

"Since when are you so concerned about Del?"

"These are Del's interests. His interests are my interests—yours too when it comes down to it."

Mickey stared at the wall of money. His mouth was dry. He turned to her. "When is this supposed to happen?" he asked.

"Tomorrow," Sharma said.

"God," Mickey said.

She pulled one of the plastic bags out of the cavity. She set it down, pulling at the tie holding the bag closed. She emptied its contents, hundreds of bills floating in the air before fluttering to the floor.

"What the hell are you doing?" Mickey demanded.

Instead of answering, she turned to face him, undoing her robe. She was naked beneath it. She dropped the robe and kneeled on the floor, lying back, stretching out on her makeshift bed of money. "Come here, Mickey," she murmured. "Come with me and we float on all the money in the world."

God he was weak, he thought, dropping his jeans.

Weak. So goddamn weak…

32

Sharma insisted on driving her Porsche to Niagara Falls. Mickey sat beside her, nervously keeping an eye on the black Louis Vuitton carryall containing the hundred and fifty thousand dollars that was to be delivered to a party yet to be named. That made him even more jumpy, the jumpiness not helped by her asking if he was armed.

"What do you mean, armed?" he asked.

"What do you think I mean? Did you bring your gun?"

"Why would I bring a gun?"

"Because you're a policeman; policemen carry guns," she answered, as if that made all the sense in the world.

"If I need a gun for this then we're both in a lot of trouble," Mickey said.

"Well, you never know," Sharma said sullenly.

But then, to his relief, she didn't pursue it further, as she swung onto Highway 407 gunning the Porsche west toward Hamilton.

"When are we supposed to meet this person?" Mickey asked.

"There is plenty of time," Sharma answered evasively.

"That's not answering my question."

"Stop being a policeman," she said. "Today you are not a policeman. Today you are supporting the woman you care about."

Did he care about Sharma? He thought of Reagan. He cared about her. Sharma? That was sex—and maybe trouble.

What was it about sex that it was always trouble?

Sharma guided the Porsche across the Burlington Skyway Bridge and then came off the Queen Elizabeth Way into Niagara Falls. Clifton Hill—"the street of fun at the Falls"—dipped down to the Niagara River and the trio of iconic waterfalls all but lost in a hazy mist.

They drove past cheesy attractions Mickey thought had died with his childhood—his parents' childhood, for that matter. But along the street of fun, they somehow survived, apparently timeless: Ripley's Believe It or Not museum; a Guinness Book of World Records exhibit; Dracula's Haunted Castle; Frankenstein—"Niagara's most terrifying experience"; a Midway; a wax museum; a sky wheel, spinning lazily against a gray sky.

The Porsche turned onto the Niagara Parkway and he found himself confronted by a wonder of the world mankind had been unable to screw up. Mickey felt suddenly like a child again, experiencing the thrill of the Falls for the first time. That feeling almost made the trip worth it.

Almost.

Except for Sharma. Sharma who was trouble. Sharma who wanted to know if he brought a gun.

Jesus Christ, he thought.

She parked in the enormous lot at the end of the Falls. Mickey slung the carryall over his shoulder, and together he and Sharma strolled the pedestrian walkway running alongside Horseshoe Falls. Sharma squealed when a burst of misty rain flew at them, taking his hand, giggling, allowing him for a few minutes to believe they were a couple escaping for a weekend in the place that advertised itself as—or maybe it didn't any longer—the world's Honeymoon Capital.

But then they passed the Sheraton on the corner of Clifton Hill. Sharma sobered and became tense.

"What's the matter?" he asked.

"It's all right," she said, pulling her hand away.

Her cellphone sounded. She stared at the screen as though uncertain whether to answer.

"You okay?" Mickey asked.

"Yes." She put the phone to her ear. "We're here," she announced to whoever was on the line. "At the Sheraton." Pause. "Okay."

"What is it?" Mickey demanded as she shut down her phone.

"I'm to leave the money in a car at the Travelodge up the street," she said.

"Who? Who wants you to leave it?"

"This is the way they want to do it, so let's go," she said, and started away before he could object.

They trekked up Clifton Hill to the Travelodge, a two-tiered structure surrounding a courtyard that doubled as a parking lot. Mickey said, "Where are you supposed to leave it."

"A blue Buick Encore."

Mickey searched around the courtyard. A blue Buick was parked at the end. "There it is," he said.

"Let's get this over with." She led him across to the Buick and came to a stop. She was breathing in short, sharp breaths.

"Open the back," Sharma ordered. "Put the bag inside."

Mickey tried the hatchback. It swung up into an open position. "You're just going to leave a bag full of money sitting here?"

"Do it, Mickey. Please. Don't argue."

He sighed, unslung the bag from his shoulder and dropped it into the back. That's when he saw the second black carryall.

"Pick that up," Sharma ordered.

He looked at her. "What's in it?"

"Just pick it up so we can get out of here," Sharma said.

He lifted the carryall out. Sharma closed the hatchback. She looked strangely at Mickey. The look unnerved him.

"What?"

She began to back away from him as he held the carryall. A man wearing a blue windbreaker appeared, crouching, pointing a Glock pistol at Mickey. Then a second man materialized, also aiming his Glock at Mickey. And then a third. And a fourth. And abruptly, the parking lot filled with men and women in blue windbreakers, everyone screaming out a cacophony of orders, few of which Mickey could understand. They seemed to be saying something about dropping the bag. He did that. Then someone yelled for him to get down on his knees. Down on the ground.

He fell to his knees, raising his hands. Other hands shoved him roughly down on the pavement, yanking his arms behind him. He heard the ratcheting click and felt the cold metal of the handcuffs closing around his wrists.

He was lifted roughly to his feet. He saw Sharma being hustled away. He saw a familiar face at the edge of the mob of law enforcement.

Adam Machota met his eyes briefly before turning away.

33

Niagara Regional Police Service headquarters was a drab box warning the miscreant not to enter.

Too late for that, Mickey thought as two uniformed officers placed him in an interrogation room, done in the same gray tones as the outside of the building.

They left him handcuffed, seated on a molded-plastic chair designed for maximum discomfort. Now there would be a waiting period, time to give the suspect—him—a chance to stew in his own juices and get good and scared. Well, he didn't scare so easily, although they had certainly shaken him. No matter how calm he remained, no matter how well he could anticipate the process, he knew he was in a shitstorm of trouble.

Sure enough, after an hour, the door opened and in stepped a large, gray-haired woman dressed in—he could hardly believe it—a gray pantsuit. Everything around here matched, he thought.

The woman seated herself across from him and smiled a grandmotherly smile before she announced, "Sergeant Dann, my name is Inspector Jill Lowry. I'm with the Royal Canadian Mounted Police."

That surprised him.

"You're not local," Mickey said.

The observation received no comment, only another grandmother-like smile. "Sergeant, you are being charged with possession of illegal opioids for the purposes of trafficking."

"Is that what was in the bag?"

"I think you know that, Mickey—do you mind if I call you, Mickey?"

"Yes, I do mind," he said, trying to keep his temper in check. "This is bullshit."

"Sergeant Dann, I'm going to give you the following warning. You need not say anything. You have nothing to hope from any promise or favor you may receive here, and nothing to fear from any threat whether or not you say anything. Anything you do say may be used as evidence. Do you understand?"

"Yes," Mickey replied.

Inspector Lowry continued: "You have the right to retain and instruct counsel without delay. You can make a telephone call at any time. Do you understand that?"

"Yes, I do," Mickey said.

"Now, you can call a lawyer or you can talk to me first and we can try to clear this up together."

"Talking to you isn't going to clear up anything," Mickey said.

"I'm sorry you feel that way," Jill Lowry said. "Do you wish to call a lawyer?"

"I want to make a phone call."

———

Jean was in her sweats pouring herself a glass of wine, debating whether to binge on a season of the

BBC series, *In the Line of Duty*, when her cellphone rang. She saw that it was Mickey Dann. What was he doing calling at this time of night?

"Hey," Jean said when she opened the phone.

"Listen, I'm in trouble," he said.

"Where are you?"

"I'm in Niagara Falls, being held at the regional police station."

"Are you under arrest?"

"That's right," he said. "I'm going to be arraigned in the morning."

"What did they arrest you for?"

"It's a setup, but I've been charged with possession of opioids."

"What can I do?"

"I've got a lawyer lined up."

"Good."

"I'm going to need a surety, Jean. Are you able to handle that?"

"Yes, of course."

"You need to get down to Niagara Falls and be at the courthouse before 10 a.m."

"I'll be there," Jean said.

"Also, I'm going to need a ride home."

"Don't worry, Mickey."

"Something else."

"Yes?"

"This isn't a local thing. It's an RCMP sting."

"The Mounties set this up?"

"With some help from Sharma."

"Sharma? Sharma Caulder? What's she got to do with a Mountie sting operation?"

"She told me her husband wanted her to deliver one hundred and fifty thousand dollars to an associate in Niagara Falls."

"What's that got to do with you?"

"She said she didn't want to make the delivery alone. She talked me into going with her."

"How did she do that?"

"The point is, there wasn't any money in the bag she gave me when we got to Niagara Falls. There were all these pills."

"Why would Sharma do this to you?"

"I'm not sure, but as they were hauling me away, I saw a friend of yours."

"Who?"

"Adam Machota."

34

Mickey's bail hearing was held the following morning inside the Niagara Court House. The charges were read—four counts of trafficking in opioids, and three counts of being in possession of the proceeds of crime, one count of being in possession of property obtained by crime.

Through it all, Mickey's lawyer, Edgar St. Jude, known to everyone as Doc, retained a slightly bemused expression, as though he couldn't quite believe the misfortune being visited upon his client. The expression was available to all his clients. A small, pudgy man with thinning sandy hair, Doc wore suits that had seen better, more fashionable, days. He walked with a pronounced limp, the result of having suffered from polio as a child.

Jean had been somewhat surprised to encounter Doc outside the courtroom. She hadn't seen him since he represented her late brother.

"I'm sorry we keep meeting under these strained circumstances," Doc St. Jude said after they shook hands.

"These are the circumstances under which you usually meet a criminal defense lawyer," Jean said.

"Point taken," Doc St. Jude said with a thin smile. "How have you been, Jean?"

"Not happy seeing what's happened to Mickey."

"Yes, a curious set of circumstances, to say the least. I wouldn't have thought Mickey the sort of police officer to get himself involved in a situation like this."

"He isn't," Jean said.

"I take it you are willing to act as surety," Doc said.

Jean nodded assent. "How likely is bail?"

"The chances are good, I believe. He's a police officer who has no previous criminal record with deep roots in the Milton community. Granted, he's removed from that jurisdiction but hopefully the judge will not view that as a deterrent."

"Have you had a chance to look at the charges?"

"Quickly. Pretty slim stuff, if you ask me. But if what you say is true, and he's not the type to get himself into trouble like this, then what the hell was Mickey doing here?"

"Good question," Jean said. "He says it was a set-up. He says Sharma Caulder is involved."

"Del Caulder's wife?"

"Sharma somehow convinced Mickey to drive to Niagara Falls. She said she had to deliver a bag of money to an associate of her husband's."

"How did Mickey get mixed up with Sharma Caulder?"

"I don't know the answer to that," Jean said. "But there is a Mountie sergeant named Adam Machota who is making life difficult for me. Mickey thinks he's somehow behind this."

"You agree?"

Jean nodded again. "Mickey tried to get him out of town. This could be Machota's revenge. What I don't understand is how he got Sharma and the RCMP to go along."

"Well, for the moment, let's see if we can get him out of jail," Doc said, opening the courtroom door to allow her to go through.

Doc St. Jude proceeded to do what he had been hired to do and got Mickey out of jail with only a pro forma objection from the crown, bolstered by Jean's agreement to act as his surety guaranteeing that he would return to court for trial.

When Mickey was released, he conferred briefly with Doc St. Jude and then Jean drove him back to Milton. For a while as Jean navigated through afternoon traffic, Mickey didn't say much other than to agree he was okay, and, no, he wasn't hungry.

"Thanks for this," he said as Jean turned the car onto the QEW highway.

"He talks," Jean said.

"Sorry about that," Mickey said. "I suppose I'm trying to deal with the realization I'm the world's biggest fool."

"Not the biggest," Jean said.

Mickey threw her a look before he said, "What I can't understand is why Sharma would do this to me."

"Maybe it has something to do with the fact that you helped put her husband in prison. I mean, what were you thinking, Mickey?"

"I guess the answer is, I wasn't thinking. Or maybe it was that she made me think something else."

"Like she couldn't resist you?"

"Well," he said ruefully, "it appears she can."

"It may not just be Sharma," Jean said.

"What do you mean?"

"When they arrested you at the motel, you saw Adam Machota, right?"

"Yeah, I did. I'm not sure how he roped Sharma into setting me up and convinced the Mounties to participate."

"Somehow, he managed to pull it off," Jean said. "He's out to destroy me, and while he's at it, take you down, too."

"I'm a stupid bastard," he announced. "Serves me right if I end up in jail."

"You may be a stupid bastard," Jean said. "But you shouldn't end up in jail because you tried to help me."

"I'm out on bail, for Christ's sake. They're already texting me from headquarters wanting to set up a meeting with my union rep. I'm screwed, is what I am."

"Well, I'm not," Jean said.

"What can you do?"

"Something," Jean said.

35

After he saved her life, he said that if she ever needed help, here was the number to call.

Anytime.

She never thought she'd make that call once she returned from Afghanistan. But now she dug through her notebooks until she found where she had scrawled the number.

She wasn't certain the number would even work at this point, whether it ever would have worked. Maybe it was just something he said. A meaningless nicety. But then he was not a man who indulged in meaningless niceties.

She picked up her cellphone and punched out the 011 exit code. The country code was ninety-three. Then she carefully tapped in the nine-digit number. It rang repeatedly but no one answered. She remained on the line hoping that the call would go to voicemail.

Eventually, there was a click and some static and then a male voice spoke in what Jean thought was Farsi. Jean said, "Hello?"

The voice answered in English. "Yes?"

"I'm trying to get in touch with Major Shaar Zorn."

"Yes?"

"Is he there?"

The line went dead.

Jean couldn't believe it. She held the phone to her ear as though the voice might magically come back to life. But it didn't.

She closed the phone.

Well, at least the number worked, she thought. She set the phone to one side, thinking, okay, now what? What to do about a ruthless bastard determined to not only destroy her, but everyone around her? The thought that there wasn't much of anything depressed her. She could cry, except she wasn't going to cry, not over the likes of Adam Machota.

Then her cellphone began to make noises. The readout showed a jumble of digits. She swiped the phone open.

"Jean?" The unmistakable voice of Shaar Zorn.

"Yes, hello, major."

"Not a major now, I'm afraid."

"Are you retired?"

"Something like that."

"You said to call if I was ever in trouble."

"Where are you?"

"I'm in Milton, Canada."

"Where you grew up, if I'm not mistaken."

"That's right. I'm living back here."

"I understand you are no longer with the RCMP," Shaar said.

"Thanks to Adam Machota."

"Yes, I understand."

"That's why I'm calling you. He's the trouble I'm in."

"Tell me," Shaar said.

"He's in town, threatening me. I believe he burned down my house. He's managed to frame the one police officer who tried to help."

"What would you like me to do?"

"I would like you to help me stop him."

The line went dead.

A white van was in the drive when Sharma got back to the house. Where did that come from? Was it Adam's? What was he doing with a van? She collected the groceries from the back of the car, including the sirloin steaks she had had cut for her new friend, Sergeant Adam Machota.

What was it with her and men in uniform? Mickey was a shit; Adam was, well, what was Adam? Remote, slightly mysterious, highly attractive. Maybe a shit, too. Maybe not.

Possibly a shit. But an exciting shit.

Thinking about this, Sharma entered the house. The young woman in the living room brought her to a stop. She wore tight leather pants and a top with a scooped neckline. The young woman was preoccupied with the TV remote control. When she sensed Sharma in the room, she looked up from the control. "I can't get this to work. Can you give me a hand with it?"

"Who are you?" Sharma demanded.

"I mean everywhere you go, there's a different remote that you can't figure out how to work. Like sometimes there are two or three of them. Crazy, huh? They should make them a lot easier."

"What are you doing here?"

The woman stopped maneuvering the remote and focused a smile on Sharma. "You must be Sharma. Right? You don't have Netflix, do you?"

"How did you get in here?"

"I'm Reagan, incidentally. I guess I should mention that. I work with Adam."

"You work with Adam? Are you a police officer?"

That made Reagan snort with laughter. "Are you kidding?"

"Then what are you doing with Adam?"

Reagan shrugged. "I'm not his girlfriend, exactly, although that's sort of how it started out. So, I guess you might as well say I work with him in this secret operation the two of you are involved in."

A big, muscular man entered the room holding a beer can. He had a face like old leather, tattoos up and down his ripped arms and biceps, a gold earring and a silver skull ring. He stopped when he saw Sharma. "Who the hell are you?"

Sharma blinked, speechless that she could be asked such a question in her own home. Reagan intervened, rising from the sofa. "This is Sharma," she offered.

"Adam didn't say nothing about anyone named Sharma," the big tattooed guy said.

"This is Richard," Reagan said, indicating the man who seemed to take up too much of the room simply by standing there. "Everyone calls him Moose."

Moose wandered past Sharma saying to Reagan, "You get that remote working yet?"

Reagan nodded at Sharma. "I'm hoping she can help us."

"Goddamn remote," Moose said, addressing no one in particular. He took a swig of his beer. "Where's Adam?"

"She thinks I'm a cop," Reagan said to Moose.

"Jesus," said Moose, shaking his head. "Spare me."

"Tell me where he is," Sharma demanded angrily.

Reagan looked offended. "Hey, take it easy. No need to get nasty."

"This is my house. Where is Adam?"

Reagan made a jerking movement with her thumb. "Upstairs, on the phone." She gave a knowing look. "Secret business."

Sharma turned and started out of the room. Reagan called after her, "You sure you can't help us with the remote?"

———

Sharma found Adam pacing back and forth in her bedroom, cellphone pressed to his ear. "Sure, if that's what you want. Let's meet then." He caught sight of Sharma, and his face twisted into an expression of displeasure. "Look, I've got to go. Yeah. Yeah. I'll deal with it."

He swiped the phone closed and turned to confront her. "What's up?"

"What's going on? Who are you?" The words burst out of her so angrily and with such speed, for a moment they didn't register with him.

"Did you hear me?"

"Of course, I heard you, I'm standing right here," Machota said.

"And who are those people downstairs?"

"They're associates of mine," Machota answered. He didn't like this line of questioning, but for now, he made sure to keep in voice level.

"You just bring them into my house with no explanation, no nothing?"

"I didn't think you'd object."

"You didn't think I'd object?" She looked at him in astonishment. "Tell me who you are and what those people are doing in my house."

"I told you before, this is an undercover RCMP operation," Machota said patiently. "You saw part of it unfold in Niagara Falls. There is more to come. The people downstairs are operatives aiding in the investigation."

"Aiding in what investigation exactly? That young woman, Reagan or whatever, she laughed when I suggested she might be a police officer. She thinks she's your girlfriend."

"That's not the case," Machota said.

"Then what is the case?"

"Right now, Sharma, you're going to have to be patient. I can't always be as forthcoming as I'd like to be."

Sharma sensed someone behind her and swiveled around to see Moose leaning in the doorway, still holding the beer. "Everything okay, chief?"

"Get out!" Sharma screamed. "Get the hell out!"

"Hey, watch it lady." A dark, murderous expression flattened Moose's face. He moved toward her, abruptly very dangerous. A cold stab of fear ran through Sharma's body.

"All right, let's not get carried away," Machota said, his voice tightening.

"Carried away?" Sharma pivoted to Machota in a fury. "This man just threatened me in *my own house!*"

Machota reacted by slapping her hard across the face. She cried out and fell back on the bed. Machota hovered over her. "Shut up! Just shut up!"

Sharma held her hands against her face, rolling onto her side, trying to stifle sobs. Machota blinked a couple of times, backing away from the bed, taking a deep, calming breath. "Jesus," he said. "If there's one thing I can't stand it's a complaining woman."

"What is this bullshit, anyway?" Moose spoke angrily. "What's going on?"

Machota swung to Moose, jabbing a forefinger at him. "And you, show a little more respect, you understand?"

"Yeah, right, chief," Moose said, his voice reduced to a sullen mumble.

"Get out of here," Machota said to Moose. "Let me deal with this."

Moose appeared to grow bigger and darker and more threatening, and for a time it didn't look as though he was going anywhere. Then he said, "I need another beer, anyway."

———————

Reagan, having listened to the commotion above, stood at the bottom of the stairs as Moose came down. "Did he hit her?"

"Yeah, well, sometimes women get what they deserve," Moose said. He went past her into the living room, draining the rest of his beer. Reagan trailed after him.

"He's crazy, you know," Reagan said.

"I don't know anything," Moose replied in irritation. "All I know is there's a job to do, and I'm doing it."

"You still believe that shit about him working undercover? Come on, Moose, get real."

"If he's not doing that, then what's he doing here?"

"Jean Whitlock, she's what this is all about. Didn't you wonder when he got you to burn down her house?"

"It was part of this operation. He got her out of there, didn't he?"

"Moose, for God's sake. What kind of undercover operation requires you to burn down a woman's house?"

"What the hell else would it be?"

"I'm not sure," Reagan said. "Something she did to him in Afghanistan, I think."

Moose shook his head. "I can't figure any of this. He hates her. He loves you. He hates you. He loves that chick upstairs. Then he slaps her around. I don't know what to believe."

"Believe that we're not in a good place," Reagan said. "Now we've invaded some woman's house and he's upstairs beating her up. Not good."

"What about that guy?"

That stopped her. "What about him?"

"You still seeing him?"

"What difference does that make to anything?"

"I'm getting a beer." Moose went past her.

She took a deep breath and then followed him into the kitchen. She found him with the fridge door open, peering inside.

"Have you said anything to Adam?"

Moose pulled another beer out of the fridge and gave her a look. "I'm no snitch, okay?"

"I appreciate that, Moose."

Moose leaned against the counter, snapping the tab on the beer can. "But if you're still seeing him, I'd go careful. I didn't say shit, but the fact he wanted me to follow you in the first place means he's suspicious."

"I know that. Believe me."

"But you're cool with me," Moose said. "It's your business. All cool."

No, it wasn't, Reagan thought. Nothing was cool.

36

A shadow in the darkness. The blurred outlines of a figure looming into focus: Major Shaar Zorn, index finger against his lips.

For a wild instant, she thought she must be back in Kandahar, and here was Shaar Zorn to wake her up for the early-morning mission into the Afghan countryside.

But no, this was not Kandahar, but it *was* Shaar, still in shadow, backing away from the bed. "Get dressed," he said softly. "Let us talk downstairs."

And then he was gone.

She got out of bed, quickly replacing her pajamas with a T-shirt and shorts, in the bathroom splashing cold water on her face. The genie had popped out of the bottle to grant her wish much faster than expected.

But what wish? Damn good question, she thought as she dried her face.

She found Shaar in the living room, unchanged since she last saw him in Kandahar: compact, muscular with a trimmed mustache and short-cropped black hair. No uniform tonight, though. For the first time since Jean knew him, the Afghan police major wore civilian dress: khaki pants, a short-sleeved cotton shirt, soft-soled shoes. Without the uniform, he looked less imposing, not so much Afghanistan's most feared cop, more like a middle-aged businessman who worked out a lot. But then thinking of Major Shaar Zorn as anything but very dangerous was a mistake.

"I didn't know if you would come or not," she said.

"I would appreciate a cup of coffee," Shaar said.

"Of course."

"I like that about you, corporal," he said with the smile she remembered, warmer than you might expect from such a cold, calculating individual. "You do not panic. A man breaks into your house in the middle of the night, enters your bedroom, and you agree to make coffee."

"It all depends on the man breaking in. For you, it's coffee."

"Black," he said, "and as strong as you can make it. I dislike your weak American coffee."

When she finished brewing the coffee, she brought him a mug and then poured one for herself. "So, how are you, Jean?" he asked after taking a sip.

"How's the coffee?"

"It will do." He took another sip and then looked at her expectantly.

"Obviously, I'm in trouble or I wouldn't have called you for help," Jean said.

"The house next door."

"My house."

"Machota?"

"I think so, yes," Jean said.

Shaar drank more coffee and then said, "Sergeant Machota should never have left Kandahar."

"You wanted him dead." Jean made it a statement, not a question.

"Sergeant Machota was involved in certain illegal activities. There were people in Kandahar who didn't like that."

"What sorts of activities?"

"The export of opiates."

"Machota? You're not serious," Jean said, genuinely surprised.

"Machota was part of a rogue group consisting of law enforcement officials from the United States, Great Britain, and Canada who found it much more lucrative to involve themselves in the drug trade rather than help the Afghan people. Unfortunately for him, Machota got into trouble with Mohammad Atta, the country's most powerful drug lord. It was Atta who decided that Machota had become a liability."

"But Machota was leaving the country."

"To set up the network needed for the movement of pills to Canada and the United States. Mohammad Atta disliked Machota, didn't want this man representing his interests in North America and so decided to have him assassinated."

"With help from you."

Shaar busied himself with the coffee. Setting his cup to one side he said, "I would not have chosen my house for Mohammad's actions, but perhaps I had no choice."

"What about now, Shaar? Do you have a choice now?"

Shaar gave her a wintery smile. "I am here to help you."

"To finish what Mohammad Atta started in Kandahar."

The wintery smile widened. "Hopefully, with less interference from you this time."

"Does that mean you have a plan?"

Shaar rose to his feet. "He's in love with you."

"Who's in love with me?"

"Machota."

For a few seconds, Jean didn't say anything in response. Then she said, "I find that hard to believe."

"Trust me. He is a man in love."

"Shaar, he's tried to kill me. He's burned down my house."

"I suspect he's done these things and more in order to get you to do what you have done."

"Which is?"

"Summon me here. It's me they are after, not you. He doesn't want you hurt, but at the same time, he knows that the only way to get at me is through you."

"But why are they after you?"

"Because I am a danger to them. You ask about a plan. Simple. The way to get to Machota is through you. You are the plan, Jean. You are how we will defeat him."

"And how will we do that?"

"You need to meet with him. Talk to him."

"I'm not sure I can."

"Yes, you can. When you meet, you must make him believe you are a possibility, that his dream of you can become a reality."

"Supposing I do this. Then what?"

"What you want done. What you brought me here to do—end your nightmare."

"Even if you are right—and I have my doubts—and I go along with this, I wouldn't have a clue how to get in touch with him."

"It's quite simple," Shaar said. He reached into his pocket and withdrew a slip of paper. He placed it on the end table beside her. "You make a phone call."

And then he was gone.

37

The fading sun added to the bleakness of the driving range. The peeling wood shed looked shabbier than ever. The patchy field in front awaited the arrival of the living dead.

Adam Machota leaned against the side of his SUV. He lifted his head, enjoying the warmth of the sun on his face. He was standing like that when the car drove in and stopped a distance from where he had parked.

Machota waited while the figure inside clambered out. Machota was determined not to move. To hell with him, he thought. Let him do the walking. Machota would enjoy the sun.

Shaar Zorn took his time, surprising Machota all over again at his shortness. Somehow, Shaar always managed to give the impression of height and authority. Machota reminded himself that he should not be fooled by the man's size. He was a son of a duplicitous bitch, never to be underestimated.

"Sergeant Machota," Shaar said, holding out his hand.

"Major Zorn," Machota answered, taking Shaar's hand in his.

"It's been a long time," Shaar added.

"Not since your people tried to kill me in Kandahar," Machota said.

"Not my people, but a misunderstanding," Shaar said.

"An interesting way of putting it," Machota said.

Shaar looked around. "What is this place."

"It's a driving range," Machota said. "Closed for the season.

"A driving range? Driving what?"

"For golfers," Machota explained. "You come out here and you hit golf balls."

Shaar looked amused. "A curious pastime."

"But a good place to meet when you don't want to be seen," Machota said. "Have you been in touch with Jean?"

"Not yet," Shaar said. "I thought I'd talk to you first."

"The story is you have come to help her," Machota said.

"And that will allow you to kill me," Shaar said.

"The fish is out of the water and therefore vulnerable."

"But you and I know something very different, yes?"

"We do."

"Or do you plan to kill me?"

"Jill Lowry is an impediment to us moving forward with your people in Kandahar," Machota said. "With her out of the way, things will be much better."

"With you in control and not having to answer to her."

"I run operations from here. You are in charge of Kandahar. A win-win arrangement for both of us."

"Yes, that's a very common phrase over here, isn't it?"

"What do they say in Afghanistan?"

"Something like, watch your ass."

Machota let out a laugh. "Yeah, good advice no matter what country you're in."

"The question is, sergeant, can I trust you?"

"Well, major, can I trust you?"

Both men were reduced to silence. They stood together in the sunlight, each refusing to take eyes off the other.

"Good," Shaar said, finally. "We are both suspicious. That will keep us honest with each other."

"Yes," Machota said.

His cellphone made chiming noises. He removed it from his pocket and looked at what was on the screen: Jean Whitlock.

Despite himself, he felt his heart leap.

Shaar said, "Do you have to take that?"

Machota shook his head. "No. It's all right."

He shoved the phone back in his pocket.

38

So, this was how you fight your enemy: you make a phone call.

Except the enemy hadn't answered. What's more, the enemy had chosen not to return the call. So much for starting a fight.

These thoughts filtered through her mind as Jean ran along the Mill Pond footpath. She was not certain whether to be disappointed or relieved. The idea of having to embrace Adam Machota, even in the name of survival, made her stomach churn. Yet if Shaar Zorn was right, and this was the path to the endgame, how could she not follow it?

She thought of calling him back, but that didn't make sense. Suddenly, she's chasing the enemy around? No, if Shaar Zorn was right, and Machota was in fact a man in love, then he would call.

Wouldn't he?

"Hey!"

Jean pulled herself out of her reverie to see Tara Ryan, in shorts that emphasized the length of her legs. Jean pulled to a stop. "Hello, Tara."

"Jock said you ran here," Tara said.

"Did you talk to the police?" Jean asked.

"I came out here yesterday and the day before, too," Tara said, ignoring the question.

"Tara, answer me. Have you talked to the police?"

"Jock says I don't have to talk to the cops. He's not going to press charges, but he says I should talk to you."

"I don't care what Jock says. That wasn't the deal."

"Cameron's scared shitless, you'll be glad to know. He's disappeared. I have no idea what's happened to him. You really screwed up my life."

"You screwed up your own life, Tara. With help, apparently, from Cameron. And no matter what Jock tells you, it's only going to get worse if you don't go to the police."

"I still need to talk to you," Tara said.

"Okay, let's talk," Jean said. "How about a coffee?"

Tara nodded assent.

———————

A product of that vast combination of disappearing small towns swallowed by the furious growth of the endless suburbia known as the GTA—the Greater Toronto Area—Tara was born in Oakville, raised in one of the anonymous developments Del Caulder had built north of the town center, her father a dentist, her mother a stay-at-home mom.

Nothing particularly remarkable about Tara Ryan, Jean decided. A young woman who discovered in public school she was a better athlete—excelling in running and gymnastics—than she was a student. In high school a further discovery—boys were attracted to her. Bundled with her athleticism that turned out to be a perfect mix for happily navigating through adolescence.

She didn't have the marks or the interest for university, but community college worked for her, a degree in sports and health sciences and what more or less passed for a career as a personal fitness trainer. She had been engaged to another trainer, but that hadn't lasted. Neither had Cameron, as it turned out.

"He was okay, I guess," Ryan explained, "Then he turned out to be a little more dangerous than I expected, a guy who lived on the edge a bit, not the typical jerk who only wants a wife in a townhouse, producing babies."

"Jock Whitlock and Desiree, were they part of life on the edge?"

"I guess that doesn't look very good, right?" She met Jean's gaze head on.

"You mean blackmailing your lovers? No, I'm afraid it doesn't."

"I mean, that wasn't the intention or anything. At least not on my part. I didn't think much past the sex, frankly. Desiree was the first time I'd been with a woman, so it wasn't as though I was out looking for something like that. It just happened, and it sort of turned Cameron on, so it was all right."

"You met Desiree first?"

Tara nodded. "At the gym. Where else? We went out for coffee—like this. And things sort of happened from there."

"And Jock?"

"You know, Desiree talked so much about him, that he actually started to sound kind of interesting. Then Cameron got some freebee tickets to a show at the Milton Arts Center, and so we went, and Jock was there, and we were introduced. I don't know how he did it, but somehow he got my number, and a couple of days later, he called and said he was interested in getting back into shape, and was I interested in working with him."

"And you were."

She moved her shoulders around and made a face. "I didn't know. I guess I was naïve, but I thought he was just someone who wanted a personal trainer. It happens all the time."

"Did you tell him about Desiree?"

"Are you kidding? I mean, I guess I mentioned that I had seen her around the gym. After all, she's hard to miss—or *was* hard to miss." She lowered her eyes, as though to honor Desiree's memory.

"But he didn't know."

"Funny, thing is, after we, you know, got together, he said his wife was having an affair, so he didn't feel so guilty about being with me. I guess I thought it was all kind of weird, but I was caught up in it, feeling kind of trapped by the whole thing, because now Cameron knew what was going on, and he saw these possibilities, you know, for getting money out of the two of them."

"Enjoying it?"

"I don't know. Cameron kept at me to keep seeing the two of them. I suppose I wouldn't have done it if I didn't sort of get off on it. I mean, listening to the two of them complain about each other, suspicious of each other, kind of exciting."

"Cameron said you were the one who wanted to get money out of them."

"That's bullshit," she flared. "I didn't even know he had phoned her. At first, I was furious, but then he said it was like twenty-five thousand dollars and all he had to do was pick up the money. He's from Erin, near Acton, so he thought that would be a good place to meet her and get the money."

"Did he tell you she was dead when he got there?"

"That's what he told me, yeah. He was pretty freaked out, and just took off. I guess you found the body."

"Did he take the money?"

"I guess he did. He never said anything about it. And now he's gone."

"When you were seeing Desiree, how was she?"

"I'm not sure what you mean."

"In the days leading up to her death. Did she seem worried? Concerned? Afraid of something?"

"That's the thing," Tara said. "We weren't even seeing that much of each other by then. The last time I actually spent time with her was about three weeks before she died. She seemed okay, I guess. A little distracted, impatient with me. I thought she was losing interest. You know, she had tried the girl-girl thing, and it was okay, but it was time to move on."

"How did you feel about that?"

"A little hurt," Tara ventured, after thinking about it. "But, you know, it's not as though I was in love with her or anything. We didn't have a lot in common other than the sex, and she was self-absorbed—I mean, *really* self-absorbed."

"But things were okay with Jock?"

"Let's put it this way," she said with a rueful smile. "It didn't seem like he had tried the boy-girl thing and had decided to move on."

"Did you know he was also seeing someone else?"

"Other than his wife?" She looked vaguely surprised. "No, but it wouldn't have made any difference. What was going on between us didn't have a whole lot to do with fidelity."

"When the two of you got together, where did you go? To a hotel or motel?"

Tara vehemently shook her head. "Are you kidding? I wouldn't do that." As though checking into a hotel with one's lover was unimaginable.

"Then where?"

"He has a place in the country no one knows about."

"Do you have a key?"

"Yes."

"Let me have it."

Tara looked even more nervous. "I'm not sure I should do that."

"Do you want me to help you or not?"

A nod this time, not quite as vehement.

"Then get the key for me."

Tara hesitated.

"Tara."

She shrugged and sighed. "I guess I don't need it "

"No, you don't," Jean said.

39

Mickey wasn't going to call. He was in enough trouble with women. But then he thought about it and the next thing he was calling her and she was agreeing to meet him at his townhouse. After that, it didn't take long for the two of them to end up in bed.

When they finally finished with each other, Reagan curled against him and said, "Well, that was nice."

"Nice?" Mickey Dann asked.

She ran her nails across his chest. "Great."

"That's better," Mickey said with a smile.

"Really great." She kissed his mouth.

"We should do something other than end up in bed together," Mickey said.

Reagan looked up at him. "Yeah? What would you like to do?"

"I don't know, what do couples do? Go to a restaurant. A movie. You know. Couples stuff. A date."

"Are we a couple?" Reagan had lifted herself up on an elbow.

"Are we?"

"I don't know. I don't know anything anymore. Like I told you, there's a problem."

"This mysterious guy you're with."

"I don't know how mysterious he is, but, yeah, the guy."

"Tell him it's over. Tell him you're seeing me."

"I can't."

"No?"

"He'd kill me. And you, too."

"I'm a cop. I can protect you."

"Are you sure about that?"

"Nobody's going to kill anybody."

"You don't know this guy," Reagan said.

"No, I don't," Mickey agreed. "So, why don't you tell me about him."

Reagan sat up, looking troubled. "I don't know how much to tell you. How much telling you will get me into more trouble than I'm already in."

"Trust me, Reagan. You won't get into trouble, at least not with me."

Her eyes searching his. "You say that now. After I tell you things, you might not feel the same way."

He reached out to her. "Don't worry," he said softly. "Nothing's going to happen to you. I'll make sure of that."

"Adam Machota," she said.

Mickey's face crossed with confusion. "What about him?"

She hesitated before she said, "He's the guy."

———————

After he settled somewhat and digested what she had told him, he asked, "How did you get mixed up with that bastard?"

"I've asked myself that a million times lately," she answered. "The easy explanation is that he caught me doing something I shouldn't have been doing in Vancouver. He let me off, providing I went along with an undercover operation he was heading in Toronto and Niagara Falls."

"An undercover operation? What kind of undercover operation?"

"He said the less I knew the better. But if I cooperated then he would make sure I didn't end up in jail."

"What did he want you to do?"

"Pose as a couple."

"Just pose?"

She grimaced. "It got to be more than that, and for a time it was okay. But then he got mean and weird—or maybe he was always mean and weird, but just hid it for a while. Anyway, after we got here I began to suspect this wasn't what he said it was." She stopped as though debating about what to say next.

"What?" he demanded.

"I found out something I wasn't supposed to find out."

"What was that?"

"That thing in Niagara Falls? That was Adam. Trying to get you out of the way. He got this Sharma woman involved."

The revelation stunned Mickey. "Wait a minute. Machota couldn't have pulled that off by himself. He'd have to be supported by other RCMP members."

"I don't know anything about that," Reagan said. "But he was out to get you."

"Jesus Christ," Mickey said. "Do you have any idea what you're saying?"

"You're starting to scare me," she said.

"You're scaring me," Mickey replied. "If what you say is true—Christ, it doesn't make sense."

Reagan looked confused. "What? I don't understand?"

"To arrest me in Niagara Falls, he would have had to involve the RCMP brass, and then had help planting shit in the car."

Reagan couldn't resist a sly smile. "I guess you shouldn't have let your little head lead your big head. Or is it the other way around?"

"Shit," Mickey said.

"Like, I'm always amazed what you can accomplish just by screwing a guy."

"Why don't you get dressed?" Mickey swung his legs over the bed. "I'll make some coffee."

She pouted. "Now you're pissed."

"No," he said, standing. "I'm glad you're being honest."

In the kitchen, Mickey poured water into the coffee maker, thinking that maybe it wouldn't be so easy to protect Reagan after all, let alone himself, and that what she knew could potentially open up a shitstorm.

It could also get her killed.

Mickey was thinking this when Reagan appeared, dressed now, wrapping her arms around his waist. "Am I in a lot of trouble?" Her voice was muffled against his back.

"It's going to be all right."

"The thing is, when people say that, it never is."

"Where is Machota now?"

"You're not going to believe this."

"What?"

"We're all staying at Sharma's place. I don't think she likes it. I think she's scared of the three of us."

"The three of you?"

"He's got this tough hombre working for him. Moose. That's his name, if you can believe it. He knows about us, but I think he likes me, so he hasn't said anything to Adam."

Mickey poured coffee for the two of them. She watched him closely. "You're worried," she pronounced.

"I'll take care of this," he said.

Even to him, that didn't sound very convincing.

40

The cabin outside Belfountain, north of Toronto, stood at the end of a leafy unpaved road, nearly hidden by the encroaching forest.

The key Tara Ryan had provided Jean stuck a bit and resisted, but finally it turned and with a soft click the door swung open to another corner in the hidden life of Jock Whitlock, a mayor with a dead wife and two lovers. At last count. Not to mention this hideaway he never told anyone about. At least he never told Jean.

The surrounding trees cut off sunlight, draping the interior in gloom. There was a musty smell in the air, coming off aged furniture as dark and worn as Jock's lies. Not a happy place, Jean thought. What was Jock doing here? Screwing Tara and possibly Grace and perhaps any number of other women?

Or was there something else?

Jean threw open the curtains covering two arched windows in the living room, as though to shed more light on Jock Whitlock's increasingly mysterious life.

Something scampered across the floor, causing her to jump. A mouse disappeared under the sofa.

The pale-yellow bedroom off the living room looked freshly painted, a cheerful contrast to the cabin's gloom. The king-size bed was covered by a Mediterranean-blue duvet.

"What secrets have you hidden away in your secret love nest, Jock?" Jean asked aloud, addressing the bed. The bed didn't answer. A side drawer gave up condoms and a tube of cherry-flavored lubricant. The cocksman ready for anything. Jean closed the drawer. Sometimes you could know too much. The chance you took poking around in the places that were none of your business.

If Jock could make love in his yellow bedroom to his heart's content, why risk it all by killing his wife? An act of passion? Discovering his lover was also his wife's lover? That somehow didn't seem like Jock. But then who was Jock, anyway? She would never have suspected this remote cabin in the woods or much of anything else she had lately uncovered about him.

Every time Jean thought that there was no way Jock could do something, it turned out there was a way. So maybe murder wasn't farfetched after all.

The vibration of her phone drew Jean out of her reverie. She recognized the number and her heart jumped.

"Jean, you were calling me," said the voice of Adam Machota.

"Yes," Jean said.

"I'm delighted to hear from you," he said. "I'm so sorry I didn't get back earlier. I've been tied up."

"I called because I thought it was time to have a talk," Jean said.

"I agree," Machota said.

"Would you? Would you like to talk?"

"I've been waiting a long time for this, Jean, a chance to put our differences behind us."

"Is that what this is about, Adam? Our differences?" Jean fought to keep down the bile rising in her throat.

"I would like to put the past where it belongs—in the past, so we can move forward together."

"Let's not get ahead of ourselves," Jean cautioned. "We need to meet, talk, so that each of us knows where the other stands."

"I agree," Machota said.

"But you must come alone," Jean said. "Just the two of us."

"Of course," Machota said. "I want you to know I'm willing to do whatever it takes to make you comfortable."

He could have started by not burning down my house, Jean thought. But still, he did sound sincere. You could almost believe him. That was the thing with Machota, wasn't it? You believed until you couldn't because he was smashing your face and tearing off your clothes.

By the time you didn't believe, it was too late.

"Tomorrow," Jean said out loud. "A neutral place. In public."

"Yes, that's fine. Where would you like to meet?"

Her mind swirled? Where indeed? Where could she stomach this man? "There's a restaurant on the lake in Burlington," she said.

He agreed to that.

Jean was driving back from Belfountain when Eddie Fitzpatrick called. "Have I got you at a bad time?" he asked.

"I'm in my car, Eddie. What's up?"

"I just wanted to check in with you," Eddie said, his voice as smooth as an Irish baby's bottom. You would buy a used car from Eddie without hesitation. But could that voice convince you Jock Whitlock hadn't murdered his wife?

"Check in with me?"

"I know that you're helping us as best you can, looking into Jock's situation."

Murder transformed into "Jock's situation." Interesting, Jean thought.

"Yes, that's right."

"I wonder if you have found anything that could help us."

"I discovered a few things that won't help 'Jock's situation' at all," Jean said.

Eddie didn't respond immediately. Finally, he said, "I'm disappointed to hear that."

"It's a matter of time until the police know what I know—or maybe they know already. Either way, Jock's been keeping things secret that he shouldn't have been keeping secret."

"Perhaps you could provide with me with an example," Eddie suggested.

"He's been seeing a young woman named Tara Ryan. Tara was also Desiree's lover."

More silence. Then Eddie said, "So, there's a motive for Jock to murder his wife."

"A crown attorney could certainly look at it that way, don't you think?"

Eddie went silent again. "Anything else?"

"He's also involved with his assistant."

"Grace Travis?"

"That's been going on for some time. Grace believes that with Desiree gone, she and Jock can finally be together."

"I take it she doesn't know about this other woman."

"Not as far as I know," Jean said.

More silence. Jean could almost hear the wheels turning inside Eddie Fitzpatrick's head. "How much does Jock know of what you know?"

"He knows."

"I'd better sit down with him," Eddie said.

"That's a very good idea," Jean agreed.

"My hope is that you will continue your investigation and uncover information that helps Jock's case." Eddie picked carefully through his words.

"I'm trying," Jean said.

"Call me as soon as you have something." Before Jean could reply, Eddie was off the phone.

"Asshole," Jean said aloud.

41

Jean found Shaar Zorn waiting when she got back to the apartment. "Well, here you are," she said, annoyed that he once again had appeared out of nowhere and managed to make himself at home.

"You must forgive me, Jean. I'm afraid I have a talent for getting into places I'm not supposed to get into."

"I'm not sure I like this," Jean said. "Even if you are on my side."

"You have spoken to Sergeant Machota."

"How could you know that?" she asked, astonished.

"He's been in contact with me."

"He's been in contact? How is that possible?"

"When it comes to sides, Sergeant Machota believes I am on his."

"How could he believe that?"

"I made him believe it."

"The same way you made me believe?"

"The difference is, I *am* on your side."

"How do I know that?"

"Because I am telling you what I'm telling you."

"That's not reassuring."

"Then you simply have to trust me."

Her eyes refused to leave his. She said, "What's going on? You said they wanted to entice you here; I am used as the bait, is that it?"

"True enough, but Machota now sees things differently. Now he sees opportunity."

"What kind of opportunity?"

"To take control of everything. So that he doesn't have to answer to anyone."

"And you can help him with that?"

"That is what he believes."

"But if Machota is gone, that opens the way for someone else. And maybe that someone is you, Shaar."

He allowed the ghost of a smile. "It opens the way to destroy this insidious international network that corrupts my country. I am the good guy here, Jean."

"Are you?"

"Machota believes his conversation with you went very well. He's excited to see you again. You are the spider, Jean, and you have successfully lured the fly into your web."

"Machota is no fly," Jean said.

"With you he is," Shaar said. "With you he is vulnerable. Let us decide how we can play on that vulnerability."

"There is a place in the country."

"Yes?"

"He might be persuaded to come…"

"Are you prepared to do that?"

"I am prepared to try," Jean said.

42

Despite his reassurances that he could protect Reagan, Mickey was at a loss how to do it. If he were still an active-duty cop, action could be taken. But in the limbo of paid administrative leave, neither fish nor fowl, and on bail with restrictions, his actions were severely limited.

Therefore, he fell back on the tried and true—albeit boring—ritual of observing the suspect. There was nothing to stop him from sitting a stakeout, beyond the rising suspicion, as he waited down the road from Sharma's house, that this wasn't going to accomplish much.

At noon Mickey was thinking again about the time he was wasting, the crappiness of a misspent life sitting in too many cars watching too many assholes when Adam Machota emerged through the main gate and drove down the hill. Mickey waited for a couple of minutes and then started after him.

Sticking to the speed limit, Machota drove south to the Highway 407 turnoff. He continued west on the toll road, Mickey following.

Machota came off onto the QEW, driving south to North Shore Boulevard. He turned left onto the boulevard. Ahead, Mickey saw Machota swing into a parking lot adjacent to an elegant glass structure: Spencer's at the Waterfront.

He turned in, passing Machota as he walked toward the restaurant. A glance to the left, and he would spot Mickey slowing to find a parking spot. But Machota never glanced left. Watching in his rearview mirror, Mickey saw him enter the restaurant.

Adam Machota was going to lunch. But with whom?

There were lots of empty spaces close by to park, but that made it easier to be spotted. Mickey chose a space at the rear with a view of the beach.

Now what? Mickey thought. More sitting and waiting. His stomach made a growling noise. It had struck him many times over the years that while the bad guys were enjoying a meal in what was usually a very good restaurant, the good guy was outside, starving.

Another car entered the lot. Mickey watched it come to a stop, closer to the restaurant. After a couple of moments, the door opened and an attractive woman stepped out and started for the entrance.

Jean Whitlock disappeared inside.

No, Mickey thought. It wasn't possible. Jean could not be having lunch with the man who was trying to destroy her life.

Yet here she was.

———————

Machota was already seated by one of the big windows that looked onto a gun-metal gray Lake Ontario. The terrace below was an outdoor café in season. Today, it was deserted and windswept. The odd strollers on the beach beyond the terrace were bent against the wind.

A raw, soulless day, Jean reflected. How appropriate.

Elegant in a dark, tailored suit, a powder-blue shirt open at the collar, Machota could be mistaken for a good-looking wealth management advisor. Except she had no wealth to manage and Adam Machota was no wealth manager.

Adam Machota was a killer.

He stood and held the chair so she could slip into it, murmuring, "Good to see you, Jean."

Choosing an outfit for a luncheon with the man anxious to see you dead had turned out to be more of a challenge than she had expected. How do you dress for your killer? A skirt? Slacks? Business professional? Femme fatale contemporary? No cleavage? Or a hint—a promise of things to come?

She opted for the hint, coupled with a skirt, short, but not too short. Advertising, but subtle advertising: interested, potentially, but not throwing herself at him.

Or so she hoped.

Machota was smiling as he reseated himself. "You're looking great," he said with enthusiasm. A neutral compliment that could draw no offence. Courteous Adam, she thought. Careful Adam. If she was luring him into her web, then he was doing much the same.

Two spiders in search of the fly.

"I was about to order some wine," Machota said.

That was the cue for their server to appear. She cheerfully announced that her name was Amy, youthful, eager Amy. She would be taking care of them today. Could she bring them something to drink?

"Sparkling water for me, please," Jean said quickly.

Machota looked briefly disappointed before ordering a glass of the house red. "I feel like celebrating," he announced as eager Amy bounced away.

"Oh? What are you celebrating?" she asked.

"Let's call it our reunion. Long overdue, I might add. But welcome."

"I see," was all Jean could think to say.

"Tell me, how have you been?"

"Adam, you know how I've been." Jean couldn't keep the note of impatience out of her voice. "How I've been is the result of the way you've been acting."

Machota's smile was smooth. "Here are our drinks," he announced.

Sure enough, Amy had returned with wine and sparkling water, asking if they'd had a chance to look at the menu.

"Give us a few more minutes, will you Amy?" Machota asked. "We've been too busy getting reacquainted."

"I understand," Amy said brightly. "Take your time. Do you mind if I say this? You're a really cute couple."

"We don't mind at all, Amy. Thank you." Machota couldn't hide his pleasure as Amy went off.

"I think she's got the wrong impression," Jean said.

"Or maybe she senses a deeper truth about us," Machota said.

"A deeper truth?"

"That perhaps we got off on the wrong foot, that maybe we should wipe the slate clean and start over."

"Is that what you want, Adam?"

"Yes, I'd very much like that, Jean. What about you?"

"I don't know." She sat back, as though to get a better view of him, as though distance might provide a more accurate sense of his truthfulness—or his deception. "I'm not sure what to make of what you're telling me."

Not very far from the truth, she thought.

"I understand," Machota said sympathetically. "Listen, it's going to take time. There's a healing process that we must go through. I'm prepared for that."

The difference is, Adam, she thought to herself, I am not prepared for it.

They ordered lunch. A salad for her; a hamburger for him. And not just any hamburger, a *craft-cut* burger. Impressive. The elegant Adam Machota. Who could imagine that a hamburger marked you as elegant: Machota joking. A kid from the interior of British Columbia, he said, a tough logger's son, eating an elegant hamburger—a *craft-cut* burger—in a stylish restaurant with a beautiful woman.

"Come on, Adam," she chided. "You've long since put your childhood behind you—and this certainly isn't the first time you've eaten in a good restaurant."

"Yes, but it's the first time I've eaten in a good restaurant with you," Adam corrected. "The last time we had a meal together, it was *bulani* in Kandahar. Not very elegant."

An hour or so before you tried to rape me, Jean thought. But she said nothing, smiling at him, adding a warmth that otherwise certainly would not be there.

"As for childhood," Machota added. "Well, I wonder if any of us ever survives that experience."

"You have to get past it, Adam," Jean said. "We all do."

"Yes, you are right. My trouble is the getting past part."

She relaxed as the food arrived. The craft-cut burger included bacon, aioli and steak sauce.

When Machota lifted the burger, steak sauce dripped out, splashing onto the snowy white table cloth.

"Maybe not so elegant," Jean said.

"I tried to warn you." Machota set the burger on his plate, contemplating the sauce muddying the table cloth. "You can't take me anywhere."

"Maybe you should use a knife and fork," Jean suggested.

Machota looked appalled. "You can't eat a hamburger with a knife and fork."

"You can't eat a *craft-cut* hamburger any other way," Jean responded. "Maybe you're right. Maybe you haven't gotten past your childhood."

He picked up his fork and knife, studying them dubiously. Then he shrugged and used the utensils to attack the burger.

"Very elegant," Jean offered, watching him closely.

"I'm relieved I'm back in your good books," Machota said.

Was he back in her good books? Jean was silently appalled. At another time, she had, if she was honest, found him attractive.

Pretend, she thought. Pretend nothing had happened, that Adam hadn't done the things he had done. Pretend she viewed him the way she had the first time she met him.

Pretend.

———————

Mickey grew cramped in the car. Cramped and increasingly curious and angry. Curious to see if they really were together inside. Angry at the notion they might be.

He got out to stretch his legs. The sky had grown darker. Rain played in the rising wind. Mickey walked to the entrance, hesitated, worried about the fallout if Machota—or Jean for that matter—spotted him. Then he thought, to hell with it, and entered.

The darkening clouds outside had cast the interior in uncertain light, draining away the restaurant's glass-encased cheerfulness.

He saw them by the window a still life in the gloom, two attractive diners poised together in a romantic setting. No reservations required.

As Mickey watched, there was movement in the still life. A hand touched another hand. Jean did not move her hand. He waited to see her hand move.

It didn't.

43

When he took her hand, it made her skin crawl.
She could hardly believe she had allowed herself
to sit there while he did that. She reminded herself as
she drove home that she had only done what was necessary.

For an instant she had been charmed, she had to
concede. But then he had touched her and the feeling
evaporated. She was repulsed, almost physically ill sitting there.

Still, in the end, she was what she had set out to
be: the Trojan Horse inside Fortress Machota. The
first necessary step. So, okay, she had survived their
encounter, albeit with gritted teeth. Now what?

They had talked about seeing each other again. She
told herself she would have difficulty stomaching another meeting, tried not to think she might be lying to
herself.

Her cellphone made rumbling sounds on the seat
beside her.

"We have to meet." Jock Whitlock's voice was tight
with anger.

"Where?"

"I'm at the house."

"I'm in the car driving back from Burlington. I can
be there in an hour or so."

"Make it as soon as you can," Jock said, and then hung up.

She reached Jock's house in twenty-five minutes. He opened the door as she came up the walk and ushered her inside. He hadn't shaved, his eyes were bloodshot, as though he hadn't slept in a while.

"Let's go out on the deck," Jock said.

"What? You think they've bugged the house?"

"It's better on the deck," he insisted.

It had stopped raining, but the cold and gray persisted. Jock in shirtsleeves, seemed not to notice. His face twisted in anger. "What the hell are you doing to me?"

"I thought I was trying to help you," Jean said.

"Not by poking your nose into things that you shouldn't be poking your nose into. That's not helping, believe me."

"Have you talked to Eddie?"

"He doesn't tell me shit."

"Eddie doesn't tell you what you don't want to hear."

"Christ!" Jock was running his hand through his hair again.

"Maybe instead of getting pissed at me, you should think about being a little more forthcoming with your attorney."

"Christ!" he repeated, spending more time running his hand through his hair, reminding Jean again that this was a Jock she had not seen before.

"Have you talked to the police yet?"

"No, Eddie's been putting them off."

"It's like I told Eddie. If I found out about Grace and Tara Ryan, then it's only a matter of time before they do, too. If they haven't already."

"If I tell them what I know, then I have to implicate Tara, and I don't want to do that."

"Jock, Tara and her boyfriend were about to blackmail you."

"It's her goddamn boyfriend. He led her astray."

"Maybe so, but you can't protect her. The more you try to hide things, the more suspicious it looks."

"Shit," he said. "None of this is going to look good."

"But none of it makes you a killer," Jean interjected. "Unless…"

"What?"

"Unless you murdered your wife."

"Jean, I didn't murder Desiree."

"What about Tara Ryan? Or Grace?"

Now Jock regarded her with disbelief. "Are you kidding me? Neither of them could do something like that."

"Couldn't they? What makes you so sure?"

"This is so crazy." Jock was shaking his head.

"Grace doesn't know anything about Tara," Jean said. "She believes that with Desiree gone, the two of you are going to be together."

"That's what she told you?"

"That's what you told her, Jock. Is she lying to me?"

"Jesus, I don't know—Christ!" Jock exclaimed.

Jock, she concluded, had found himself in a place he had spent a lifetime trying to avoid: in a corner he couldn't escape. For once he could not duck and weave or simply walk away. He was trapped by his own missteps, and it was evident he didn't like it.

Jean said, "I mean it looks like she's moved in with you."

"No, she hasn't!" Even more vehement. "You've got the wrong idea about this."

"Or Grace has the wrong idea."

Jock slumped onto a nearby deck chair, seemingly exhausted by his lame attempts at denial. "Look, I'm not saying I've handled any of this very well."

"Good Jock, I'm glad you're not saying that, because you sure as hell haven't."

"Tara has complicated things as far as Grace is concerned, made me uncertain about my feelings."

"Knowing what she was up to with her boyfriend, knowing that she was also involved with Desiree?"

Jock buried his head in his hands. His voice became muffled. "God in heaven, what have I got myself involved in?"

"Nothing that's going to look good to the police," Jean said.

When he lifted his head again, his eyes had cleared; the scared murder suspect was gone. It was such a rapid transformation, Jean wondered if what went before had been a put-on; the unshaven, grieving widower, distraught and sleepless, hiding the truth from himself.

"We've got to get to work," he pronounced, the strength back in his voice.

"How do you propose *we* do that?" Jean asked. "You said it yourself. When I poke my nose into it, you end up looking worse than you did before."

"Now you know the truth, Jean. Everything is out in the open, nothing left to hide. We start over."

"If you didn't kill your wife, and Grace didn't do it, and Tara isn't the culprit, then who would have done something like this?"

Jock shrugged. "I don't know. Desiree was interested in clothes and parties and expensive restaurants. People wanted to screw Desiree, they didn't want to kill her."

"So, then maybe it's something else," Jean said.

"What do you mean?"

"Maybe whoever killed Desiree wasn't after her. Maybe she was killed to get at you."

"Who would want to do that?"

"I don't know, Jock. But you would. Who?"

And as Jock sat pondering this, Jean thought suddenly that she had the possible answer to her own question. Maybe it wasn't someone who wanted to get at Jock. Maybe the killer wanted to get at her.

An image flashed in her mind: a figure getting out of a car in an Acton parking lot.

Adam Machota.

44

Jean was spreading peanut butter over rice cakes, her daily lunch, when she heard footsteps on the stairs. That was the thing about living above a funeral home, anyone could walk in.

She stepped into the hall as Mickey Dann reached the top of the stairs. She had a chance to say, "Mickey," before he shoved her hard against the wall. "What the hell do you think you're doing?" he demanded.

She pushed him away. "You don't come in here and push me around, you bastard."

"You don't want to get pushed around, then maybe you shouldn't be having lunch with goddamn Adam Machota."

"You were *following* me?" Her eyes flared angrily.

"I was tailing Machota. I followed him to a restaurant in Burlington where, to my surprise, I find him enjoying lunch with the woman I'm supposedly trying to protect."

"I don't need your protection," Jean said.

"Apparently not. Never mind that this bastard burned down your house and has practically destroyed my life, just the guy you want to have lunch with."

"You weren't supposed to see that," Jean said, moving away into the kitchen.

"I guess not," Mickey said, trailing after her.

"Trust me, it wasn't what it seemed."

"No? Then what was it?"

She stalked over to him and slapped his face. "Don't ever push me again. Understand?" Then she kissed him hard on the mouth.

She pulled away. He looked at her uncomprehendingly. "What's the matter?" she demanded and then kissed him again. This time he returned the kiss. She put her arms around his neck, pulling him close, breathing hard.

He said something like, "What's going on?"

She didn't answer. They struggled together into the living room, shedding clothes along the way. By the time she fell on the sofa, Jean was naked. Mickey loomed over her.

She pulled him down to her.

———————

Much later, curled together, framed in what was left of the daylight seeping through the windows facing James Street, Mickey said, "I should tell you."

"What?"

"I've wanted to do that since we were in high school."

"I guess I should ask, what took you so long?"

There were a thousand complicated answers to *that* question. Mickey avoided all of them with a snort of laughter.

They fell silent for a time. Then she said, "It could be I was trying to distract you."

"I prefer to think you were overcome with lust."

"Yes," she said, smiling, "I suppose that's a possibility, too."

"Now what?"

She thought about it and then said, "Now we get dressed—and for the time being you refrain from asking me questions until I figure out a few things."

"So, you *were* trying to distract me."

"That's what I should be telling myself."

"But?"

She smiled. "I could be lying."

Mickey had nice eyes, Jean thought, even as they inspected her with unusual intensity. Tough guy cop, with nice eyes. Interesting combination. He said, "Here's what you don't know about your lunch pal."

"Okay," she said.

"He's holed up at Sharma's house."

"I guess I shouldn't be surprised, given what she's done to you. But how do you know this?"

"I followed him from there."

"But how did you know he was with her?"

He hesitated before he said, "Reagan told me."

"Reagan. Who is Reagan?"

"She's with Machota."

"You're seeing a woman who is with Machota?" Jean's voice was full of disbelief.

"She's scared of him. She wants to get away."

"And you're the knight in shining armor riding to her rescue."

"You sound jealous."

"I sound amazed. Sharma. Reagan. Me. There's no end to the women you've seduced."

"Hey, you seduced me, remember?"

"Did I?"

"You were out to distract me."

"Right. For a minute there, I almost forgot."

She got out of bed and started to dress. "Distraction's over for today," she announced. "Time for you to go home."

"You're throwing me out?"

"I've got things to do."

"True love didn't last very long."

"It never does," Jean said. She wrestled a T-shirt over her head. "Get dressed. I've got to get out of here."

"Mind if I ask where you're going?"

"To visit Sharma," Jean said.

Mickey groaned.

45

Inspector Jill Lowry, behind the wheel of her Range Rover, turned off the highway. As instructed, she continued on what was no more than a dirt track threading through lichen-covered granite outcroppings.

It was nearly dark when Inspector Lowry stopped her vehicle and got out, shivering, drawing her down jacket around her. With the sun gone, it was unseasonably chilly. She pulled on the mitts her niece had knitted for her last Christmas.

The forest dark and deep, Jill searched around, apprehensive, not an emotion she had felt for a long time. She shook off the feeling. She was, after all, a veteran Royal Canadian Mounted Police officer. You don't mess with the Mounties. Not even out here in these dark woods.

A tree branch cracked behind her. Inspector Lowry swung around to see Major Shaar Zorn wearing a leather jacket and a smile. Inspector Lowry liked the jacket. She was less certain of the smile.

"Hold it right there, Major." The sharp, commanding tone in Inspector Lowry's voice had been perfected over a long police career.

Shaar Zorn came to a stop and Inspector Lowry saw with satisfaction that his smile had slipped a bit. "Is there a problem, Inspector?"

"Yes, there is."

"I'm sorry to hear that." Shaar sounded solicitous.

"It may have something to do with the fact I don't like where we're meeting."

"Safely away from prying eyes—and the ubiquitous video cameras you have everywhere in North America," Shaar said.

"You said you would be in touch when you had something to report."

"I have been in contact with Machota," Shaar said.

Inspector Lowry regarded Shaar with narrowed eyes. "What do you mean? That was not part of the plan."

"Not part of your plan, perhaps, but a necessary part of mine," Shaar said. "Machota believes I am an ally."

Conflicting emotions crowded Inspector Lowry's face before settling into what she liked to think of as her expression of unconcerned authority. "Not to put too fine a point on it, Major Zorn, but the agreement was that you were going remove Sergeant Machota as an impediment to our continued success."

"You brought me here to kill him," Shaar said.

"His obsession with this woman, his refusal to move forward with the things we all agree need to be accomplished, puts us at great risk."

"I agree with you," Shaar said.

Inspector Lowry said in exasperation, "So, yes, if I have to say it in so many words, I want him dead. You promised you could make that happen."

"But he can't do that, Jill," a voice called out.

She turned to see Machota walking toward her. As calmly as she could she said, "Adam."

"You should have let me know you were going to be in the area, Jill."

"What's this about?" she demanded.

"What's it about, Jill? Unless I miss my guess, it's about betrayal," Machota said. "You ought to be ashamed of yourself."

Jill Lowry opened her mouth to say something but that's when Shaar stepped up behind her, yanking at her hair, exposing her throat so that he could cut into it with the steel blade of the pesh-kabz, the single-edged Persian fighting knife that had been in his family for generations. She struggled against him, attempted to scream, but the sound was almost immediately cut off. Blood sprayed from her jugular in a long crimson stream.

Inspector Lowry made a final gurgling sound. Shaar, holding the bloody knife, allowed her body to drop to the ground.

The last thing she ever saw was Machota. Blank-faced. Showing no emotion.

———

Dragging a dead body at night through dense underbrush proved to be more difficult than either Machota or Shaar imagined.

They reached the clearing Machota had found earlier, and where he had left the two spades hidden beneath a thin covering of leaves and brush.

"Right here," he announced.,

Shaar was sweating as he looked around. "I would have found a spot further into the forest," he said.

"Not having second thoughts, are you Shaar?"

Shaar smiled. "The trouble with second thoughts is that they always come too late. That's why I never have them."

"Then let's do this so we can get the hell out of here," Machota said.

He retrieved the spades, handing one to Shaar, and then began to dig. Shaar hung back for a time before joining in.

They labored silently in the darkness, a half-moon struggling through the surrounding trees. Finally, after they had managed to excavate a shallow cavity, Machota signaled that was enough. They rolled the body into the hollow and then went to work replacing the dirt.

When they finished, Shaar Zorn leaned hard on his shovel, catching his breath, his perspiring face having taken on a yellowish cast that alarmed Machota. "Are you okay?"

Shaar quickly straightened. "I'm fine." He indicated the gravesite. "Let's talk about what comes next," Shaar said.

"All right. What is next?"

"Jean."

Machota hesitated before nodding. "All right."

"Her uncle has a place in the country," Shaar said. "I've discussed this with her. She will soon lead you there. She will make it appear as though she wants to be alone with you, dangle the possibility that it might lead to something else."

"It's more than a possibility," Machota asserted.

"I am never certain sergeant, whether your intention is to love Jean or eliminate her."

"Maybe both," Machota responded.

"You know that's not possible."

"Then we have to eliminate her, don't we?"

"When she invites you…"

"And I rush to her country place to be at her side."

"I will be waiting."

"To take care of me."

"Yes, that's what she will think."

"But…?"

"It will not end the way she thinks," Shaar said. "Too bad. I rather like Jean."

"I love her," Machota said. "That's the difference between the two of us."

They moved off, carrying the shovels, Machota leading the way back through the woods.

For a time after they were gone, the clearing remained deserted, silent except for the whistling wind, the creak of restless tree branches.

Then a sound that did not come from the wind or the trees.

Someone moving.

46

Jean stepped out of her hiding place in the trees to stand in the clearing, listening for sounds of the two men returning unexpectedly.

There were none.

She moved toward the freshly dug mound, the disturbed earth.

She dropped to her haunches, studying the grave. They hadn't done much of a job of it. The shallowness surprised her. Two professionals who should know better if they wanted to cover up their crime. To be safe, they should have gone deeper, but the ground was rocky and nearly unyielding and they were men in a hurry.

She used her hands, clawing, clearing away the loose dirt, digging down until she uncovered enough of the corpse. The flashlight on her phone illuminated Inspector Jill Lowry's pale face. Jean could hardly believe what she was seeing.

Why would they kill her?

Unless they were all together; two of the three had decided, for whatever reason, that she was no longer necessary.

In their world, when you were unnecessary, you were dead.

But what to do about it? Call the police? The RCMP? At the moment, her trust of law enforcement didn't extend beyond this clearing. Calling in the authorities might mean that Inspector Lowry would simply disappear from this remote wood with no one the wiser.

But if she wasn't left here, if she was in a place where she could not be ignored ...

Good God, she thought, did she have the nerve to do this?

She rose to her feet, dismissing thoughts of what she could or could not do; thinking only about what she *had* to do.

It took Jean an hour to drive back to town. The funeral home was in darkness. Doris had left for the night. Perfect, Jean thought.

Inside, she hurried to the storage room where she found the coveralls she had once worn to help her father as a teenager, pleased that they still fit.

Next, she collected the items she was going to need: a spade, a portable aluminum body lifter, a first-call body cover, lap and leg restraints, a box of nitrile examination gloves.

She shoved a Streamlight ProTac tactical flashlight into a carryall, along with the other equipment and a bottle of water and an apple. She hefted the carryall onto her shoulder and went outside with the lifter. Streetlights along James Street in front of the funeral home cast the silent night in a pale-yellow glow. Jean loaded her equipment into the back of the van and then got behind the wheel.

Back at the woods, guided by the ProTac flashlight, Jean had little trouble retracing her steps to the clearing.

She turned off her flashlight, throwing the surrounding trees into relief against the glow of the moon in the night sky. The wind made moaning sounds through the trees. A mournful night, perfect for digging up bodies, Jean thought.

She dropped the carryall and the body lifter to the ground, and then unzipped the carryall to remove the spade. She pulled on a pair of the examination gloves before picking up the shovel.

Inspector Jill Lowry, streaked with dirt, lay on her back, eyes open, as though waiting to be exhumed. Glad to oblige, Inspector, Jean thought, down on her knees clearing away the remaining dirt and rock. Once that was done, Jean rose, removed the gloves, and then replaced them with a fresh pair. She set the body lifter on either side of the corpse, slipped the straps beneath and reattached them. Inspector Lowry now lay on the lifter so Jean could pull her out of the cavity. Once that was done, Jean tied restraints to the wrists and ankles so that the body would not slip off the lift.

The wood was darker, the moon having mostly disappeared behind trailing clouds. Jean slung the carryall around her and then gripped the handles, raising the body lifter so that it became a makeshift litter she could drag behind her. It was slow going having to tilt the litter in order to navigate through the labyrinth of trees.

Exhausted and sweating, Jean finally reached the van. She rested for a time, eyes on the dirt-streaked corpse of Inspector Jill Lowry, questioning again how this grandmotherly figure, this model of righteousness, ended up in a shallow grave, murdered by men who were anything but righteous.

No time to consider motives or much of anything for the time being. She opened the rear doors and then hefted the body lifter, struggling to push it into the van.

She draped Inspector Lowry in the body cover before closing the doors.

She got behind the wheel, allowing herself to breathe, forcing herself to relax. The worst was over, at least that's what she told herself. There was only one thing left to do.

Jean turned the ignition key. The vehicle came to life. Jean put it into drive and started back for Milton.

————————

At 6:30 a.m., after a fitful sleep, Jean rose and hurriedly dressed in her jogging clothes. She drank some water and did stretching exercises. Then she went out onto James street, crossing Mill to begin her run. At the end of the street, she tramped down the iron staircase to Rotary Park, moving swiftly along the asphalt path to the Mill Pond. At this time of the morning, she was alone. Not even a dog walker. That somewhat disappointed her, but that was okay. Maybe it was better if she made the discovery.

She went up the steps onto the pathway along the pond, picking up more speed until she saw the body.

And then she came to a stop.

PRESENT DAY

47

Adam Machota's phone began making musical sounds, and that brought him awake in an empty bed. He picked his phone off the bedside table and swiped it open.

"Sergeant Machota?" a stern voice inquired.

"Yes, this is Sergeant Machota."

"Sergeant, my name is Inspector Gordon Castle. I don't know if you remember me. We met briefly when you were stationed in Kandahar."

"Yes, Inspector," Machota said in a neutral voice as he desperately tried to place the name. Was he part of the team, therefore a friend? He drew a blank.

"You're still in the Milton area, is that correct?" Inspector Gordon Castle spoke in a clipped, no-time-for-chitchat voice. One of those bosses who came outfitted with a stick up his ass, Machota quickly concluded.

"That's right, sir," he replied. "I'm on assignment here."

"Who assigned you to the Milton area, sergeant?"

The question made Machota hesitate. "I'm sorry, sir," he said finally. "This is an open line. With all due respect, I don't know you—or know you well enough to be answering questions without an okay from my superior."

"That's why I'm calling. Your superior is Inspector Jill Lowry. Yes?"

"Yes, sir."

"I'm sorry to be the one to inform you that Inspector Jill Lowry is dead."

For a moment, Machota wasn't certain he had heard correctly. "I'm sorry, sir?"

"The inspector's body was found earlier this morning."

Machota felt as though his head was spinning. "Found where, sir?"

"Where you are, sergeant. In Milton."

"Are you certain of this? As far as I know, Inspector Lowry is in Ottawa."

"That's my information," Inspector Castle maintained. "An area of town known as Mill Pond. Are you familiar with it?"

"Yes, I am," Machota said.

"I have a homicide team headed there to assist the local police, but, in the meantime, I want you at the crime scene."

"Yes, sir."

"Confirm the inspector's identity and do what you can to get to the bottom of what happened. You report back to me, understand?"

"I'll get over there right away," Machota said.

"Keep in touch," Castle said. The line went dead.

Machota put the phone down. He sat on the edge of the bed, eyes closed, forcing himself to take the deep breaths that usually served to relax him. This morning that didn't work.

How could this be? How could Jill Lowry's body have ended up at the Mill Pond? He and Shaar Zorn had buried her body in woods far from Milton. And yet less than twenty-four hours later, someone managed to exhume her and transport her to town.

Who the hell would have done that?

Shaar Zorn? Would he have returned to the clearing, dug up the body, and then transported it to Milton? Who else could it be? But then...*why* would he do that?

He almost phoned Shaar, but then decided against it. If they were sending a homicide team, they would start looking at everything, even the possibility of his involvement. That could mean checking his cellphone records. Right now, he needed time to understand what had happened and once he had done that, deal with the situation.

That was going to be a whole lot more difficult with outsiders poking around, led by stick-up-his-ass Inspector Gordon Castle.

As he dressed it crossed his mind that Jean might be behind this; he immediately dismissed the notion. She couldn't have known where he and Shaar Zorn were meeting Jill Lowry. And how could she have handled the logistics involved in transporting a body?

No, forget her. Besides, so much had changed between the two of them. He thought about their lunch and that sent a surge of warmth through his body. A relationship was developing. He wanted to be with her, and he was certain she wanted to be with him.

He had to be more trusting now that she was falling in love with him.

———————

At the Mill Pond, Machota greeted the crime scene techs in their white Hazmat suits, identified himself to Walt Dunnell, the police chief, a pompous ineffectual prick, Machota soon decided. He was escorted into the tent housing the body. One of the techs opened the flap. The round smudged face staring up at him—accusingly? —belonged to Jill Lowry.

Machota forced himself to look shaken, not hard to do, given the circumstances. "Jesus Christ," he said.

"Any idea how she got here?" The bland poker-face of one of the detectives moved into his line of vision as Machota regained his feet.

"I'm sorry, who are you?"

"Detective Petrusiak," Petrusiak said. "You're Sergeant Machota?"

"That's right. I got a call from Inspector Castle."

"Yeah, I talked to him earlier. I guess this is going to turn into a federal thing, because it's one of your people."

"Castle sent me over to meet with you to understand what's happened."

"That's what we're trying to figure out. Looks like someone cut her throat."

Machota said, "That part's not hard to figure out."

"Did you know she was in Milton?"

"No idea," Machota said. "We were working together on a case, but she was coordinating it from Ottawa. I didn't know she was in town."

"What kind of case?" Petrusiak asked.

Machota could see Walt Dunnell hovering in the background. "This gets to be a sensitive issue," Machota said. "I'd better check with my superiors before saying too much about an ongoing undercover investigation."

"Undercover?" Petrusiak looked vaguely annoyed.

"That's right," Machota said.

"This is a murder, sergeant, one of your colleagues. Anything you can tell us will be helpful, particularly if what the two of you are involved in got this woman murdered."

"I understand that," Machota said. "You're undoubtedly aware that an RCMP murder squad is on its way here. I'm just covering until they arrive. As soon as I'm cleared, you'll get all the information we have."

Petrusiak still didn't look happy. He threw a quick glance at Chief Dunnell who stepped forward, an eager expression on his face. "Of course, we want to cooperate with the Mounted Police in any way we can."

"I appreciate that, Chief," Machota said. "As you can imagine, this is quite a shock. Inspector Lowry was not just my superior. She was also a good friend. I can't imagine how this happened in the middle of town in an area where there are lots of people moving about."

"The forensics people don't think she was murdered here," Chief Dunnell offered.

"They don't?" Machota looked surprised.

Petrusiak was shooting dark looks that either the chief ignored or was oblivious to. "It's preliminary, of course, but at the moment they believe the murder took place in another location and then the body was moved here."

"I wonder why someone would leave the body here?"

"That's what we're trying to ascertain," said Chief Dunnell authoritatively.

"I assume a passerby found her," Machota said.

"That's correct," Chief Dunnell agreed. "In fact—and Detective Petrusiak can correct me if I'm wrong—but I believe it was a former RCMP officer who found the body."

Machota looked at Petrusiak. "Is that true?"

"Apparently," Petrusiak said sullenly.

"A local woman," Chief Dunnell added. "Jean Whitlock. Her family has owned a funeral home around here forever."

48

"I couldn't take it any longer, I had to get out of that woman's house," Reagan said to Moose Haggerty. "I feel like we're holding her prisoner or something."

"What? You prefer this place?" Moose said, looking around the interior of the warehouse where Reagan had asked him to meet her.

"Like what is this, anyway?" Reagan asked. "What's he doing with an empty warehouse?"

"I don't know. In case we need a place to talk? Who gives a shit?"

"I'm leaving town, Moose. I don't know what's going down, but it's bad."

"We don't know what he's up to, it could be all right."

"I don't think so. I've got it on very good authority."

"Yeah, whose authority? That guy you're seeing?"

"He knows things."

"What kind of things?"

"Look, I'm trying to help you out, okay? We both got into this situation under false circumstances. The shit is about to hit the fan. I'm making my escape; you should, too."

"Yeah, well, maybe you should hold up a minute and think this through. You run and guess what, he's gonna come after you."

"I don't think so," Reagan reassured. "He's got a whole lot more to worry about than the two of us."

"I wouldn't be too sure about that," a voice said.

Reagan and Moose whipped around to see Shaar Zorn emerge from the shadows. "I'd be careful if I were you, Reagan. I think he would come after you. I know I would."

"Who the hell are you?" Moose demanded.

"My name is Shaar Zorn. You could call me an associate of Sergeant Machota's."

"What kind of associate?" Reagan watched as Moose bulked himself into threatening mode, a scary sight.

"Someone who can help him clean up the mess he has created for himself."

"Adam didn't say nothing about no associate," Moose said.

"I'm new to the investigation," Shaar said.

"Yeah, well, I don't know who you are, pal. So, until I do, I don't like you creeping around. Why don't you take a hike?"

"I'm disappointed in you, Moose," Shaar said. He didn't seem at all intimidated by Moose, Reagan observed. That scared her.

"Tough shit," Moose said.

Shaar delivered a thin smile. "You knew Reagan was sleeping with a local cop, but you failed to tell Machota. That's not good."

"I didn't know the guy was a cop," Moose said. "She's sleeping with a guy. So what? I didn't figure it was any big deal."

"This is crazy," Reagan said to Shaar. "What are you doing here? How do you even know about this place?"

Shaar focused on Reagan. "And you, Reagan, betraying Adam after everything he's done for you."

"What he's done for me? He got me into more trouble than I've ever been in—and I've been in a lot of trouble, believe me. But nothing like this. I don't owe him anything."

"Adam will be sad to hear that," Shaar said. "He's a bit torn right now, but I believe he's quite fond of you."

"The cops know all about him," Reagan said, the accusation giving her voice renewed strength. "You do anything to either of us, and they'll know. They'll know who to come after."

"I'll keep that in mind," Shaar said.

One minute the curious-looking knife wasn't in Shaar's hand, the next it was. Reagan opened her mouth to scream. But there wasn't time for a scream. Shaar slid the blade into her throat. One quick, elegant move, so fast Moose didn't realize what had happened until he saw the blood spurting from Reagan's jugular. She grabbed at her throat, staggering away, eyes bulging. She sank to her knees, blood everywhere. She reached up imploringly to Moose and then fell over and lay still in a spreading blood pool.

Moose looked down at Reagan. "What the hell," he said.

"I thought you could do better than that, Moose," Shaar said, holding the knife, barely breathing.

"Give me a moment to think of something," Moose said. Then he added, "I know."

"What is it?"

"You're an asshole. How's that?"

"Not bad," Shaar conceded. "Where I come from, most people can't get past begging for their lives."

Moose indicated the knife. "You kill a lot of people with that where you're from?"

"It's called a pesh-kabz," replied Shaar. "An Afghan death knife."

"No shit," Moose said.

"And I've killed far too many people with it."

"I won't be begging," Moose advised. "I don't beg assholes for anything."

"Good for you," Shaar said.

Moose suddenly charged at him. Shaar was ready, deftly stepping to one side, slashing with the knife.

It took Moose a moment to realize his throat had been cut open.

By then it was too late.

———————

As Shaar came out of the warehouse, his phone began to make noises. He swiped it open. Jean said, "I'm on my way."

"You're in your car?"

"Yes. Headed north."

"Good," Shaar said. "The beginning of the beginning that will take us to the end."

"I wish I was as certain as you seem to be."

"He will follow you. And when he does, I will be there."

"Where are you now?"

"Tying up some loose ends," he said. "But do not worry. I'm not far away."

"I'll see you soon," Jean said.

The line went dead. Shaar had a momentary thought something wasn't quite right. Nothing he could put his finger on.

But something.

He reached his car, struggling with his misgivings.

Not to worry, he told himself. Events were unfolding as he had planned. He got behind the wheel and started the engine.

The beginning of the beginning, he thought again. With the end not far away, an hour or so up the road.

49

The day had begun full of sunlight and promise. But this was not a day for sunlight or promise. Dark clouds turned the world the color of lead. The clouds promised rain. The clouds matched Jean's dark mood as she sped north along Regional Road 25.

She hadn't packed much, believing that however the next hours unfolded, the end would come quickly. Bottles of water, a box of granola bars, a first aid kit, three boxes of ammunition—hollow point bullets for maximum stopping power—all packed into the carryall on the seat alongside the police baton. The Ruger was jammed uncomfortably in the waistband of her jeans.

So, she was prepared. Or was she? Her stomach churned. She felt depressed and alone, driving northeast beneath a threatening sky, headed for—what? An abyss from which there might be no escape?

Quite possibly.

And even if she did make it out, then what? Her life had not amounted to much since leaving the Force. And maybe it never had amounted to anything—maybe no one's does when it comes right down to it. Except most people cover up the meaningless of it all with family, community, a job. She had none of those.

The lone survivor trusting no one, with only herself to rely on. She tightened her grip on the wheel and took a deep breath. Fuck it. She would get through.

She would survive.

Somehow.

––––––––––

Forty minutes later, as she neared the village of Belfountain, Jean could not detect anyone following her on the narrow backroads along which she had been travelling. She wasn't sure whether to be worried or relieved. Perhaps a little of both.

She pulled off a half mile from the cabin, not far from the part of the Niagara Escarpment near Belfountain that had dug itself into a deep, jagged rift in the landscape.

Jean, with the carryall slung around her shoulder, took her time climbing down to the floor of the rift. She followed it around great chunks of rock until she reached a narrow pathway that led steeply up to a narrow field fronting a wall of trees. She crossed the field and wended her way through the trees until she spotted the cabin nestled in a hollow valley. She stopped, dropped the carryall to the ground, crouched, watching the cabin.

It had begun to rain.

50

Mickey Dann had no trouble finding the ware-house complex north of the 401 Highway seeing as how the parking lot was crowded with police cars, forensics evidence vans, as well as a couple of ambulances. There was even a giant fire truck. What the hell was a fire truck doing here? Mickey wondered as he parked and got out of the car. Milton's first responders out in force, no one wanting to miss the action.

There was always an adrenalin rush at a crime scene. Most of these first responders, whether they would admit it or not, were adrenalin junkies. You lived for moments like this, Mickey thought, everyone serious and self-important, parading around in their uniforms.

He nodded to the two cops standing watch over the line of yellow tape, ducked beneath it as he spotted Glen Petrusiak coming toward him.

"This is a fine goddamn mess," Petrusiak said.

"Must be if you're calling me," Mickey said. "So, what's up?"

"I know I'm not supposed to, but I'd like you to take a look inside. Hopefully you can save us some time."

"What have you got?"

"Too many bodies," Petrusiak said ruefully. "Every time I turn around lately, someone shows up dead. What's happened to this town?"

"Something wicked," Mickey said.

Petrusiak looked at him for a moment, saw that he was serious, and then said, "Follow me."

Dust-laden shadows filled the interior of the warehouse. Ghosts in white silently measuring, photographing, collecting, floated across a concrete floor where the two bodies lay under the glare of portable lights.

There was blood everywhere, running across the cement floor. As he drew close, Mickey saw that one of the bodies was male and that the other was a female, pale against the crimson. Both their throats had been horribly cut. Then he recognized the woman.

"Jesus Christ," he said.

Petrusiak looked at him. "What is it?"

Mickey didn't say anything. He just stood, staring down at the bodies.

Petrusiak said, "You know the woman.?"

"Yes," Mickey said in a choked voice.

"Tell me who she is." Petrusiak on his professional detective high horse. Just the facts. Asshole, Mickey thought.

Out loud, he said, "Her name is Reagan Elliott. She came to town with Adam Machota."

"His girlfriend?"

Mickey answered slowly. "Something like that, I suppose."

"I just talked to Machota. The Mounties assigned him to ride shotgun when Jean Whitlock found Jill Lowry's body."

"You're kidding? They put Machota in charge?"

"Only until their homicide team got here. They arrived a couple of hours ago. Started asking a lot of questions. They want to talk to Adam Machota, big time."

"They don't know where he is?"

Petrusiak shook his head. "They've got an APB out for him."

Mickey pointed to the bodies. "They can add murder charges to whatever they've got on him."

"You think he did this?"

"Right now, he's a damned good candidate."

"I'd better get on to the Mounties." Petrusiak started away.

Mickey stared down at Reagan, fighting off something he had never experienced before at a crime scene: tears. He swallowed hard.

"Mickey."

He looked up to see that Petrusiak had stopped and turned to him. "What is it, Glen?"

"I probably shouldn't be telling you this, but the thinking around the thing in Niagara Falls has changed."

"Yeah? How's that"

"They're coming around to the idea that Machota set you up—with help from Sharma Caulder. Apparently, she is the woman scorned in the case."

"Have you talked to her?"

"I haven't, but the Mounties are in the process of doing that. We'll see."

Mickey thought of Jean. "Shit," he said.

"What is it?" Petrusiak asked.

Without answering, Mickey started away. "Hey," Petrusiak called, "where are you going?"

Outside, Mickey called Jean's number. She didn't pick up. He got into his car and drove to the funeral home. He found Doris Clapper in her office. She looked up expectantly as he entered. "Have you seen Jean?" he asked.

"I saw her leave," Doris said.

"Any idea where she was going?"

Doris shook her head. "She had a carryall with her and seemed in a hurry."

"So maybe out of town?"

Doris shrugged. "Could be, I suppose. Her uncle might know something. They've seen a lot of each other lately."

"Thanks, Doris."

He turned to leave. She called after him. "There is something."

He turned to her.

"I was watering the plants at the side of the funeral home not long ago. Jean drove in and got out of her car. She was on her cellphone and didn't see me. I think she was talking to her uncle about a place he has up north."

"Any idea where?"

"I think she said Caledon. But Mayor Jock would know for sure."

Mickey hurried out to his car. It had begun to rain.

51

Hard rain, accompanied by the rumble of thunder. Jean shifted uncomfortably. She had kept watch for the past two hours. No one had appeared at the cabin. If anyone lurked in the surrounding forest waiting to ambush her, that person had yet to show himself.

She eased up out of the crouching position she had adopted, noting the pain in her hips and lower back, age asserting itself in unpleasant ways, reminding her that squatting for long periods in the rain was not a good idea.

Hoisting the carryall onto her shoulder, she moved carefully down the hillside to the cabin. She used Tara's key to unlock the front door.

She decided not to turn on the inside lights. Instead, she positioned a straight-back chair in the kitchen area where she had a view of both the front door and the rear entrance. She pulled the Ruger from her waistband and set it on a side table beside the chair. She laid the baton next to the gun.

She unzipped the carryall and removed the water bottles, an apple and a granola bar. She drank water and then ate the apple and granola bar.

Outside, the rain poured down, driven by a fierce wind, pounding against the windows. A thunder clap startled her. Calm down, she counseled herself. It was going to be a long night.

She drank more water. There was another thunder clap, followed by much ominous rumbling. The gods must be angry this evening.

Jean could hardly blame them.

He barged past a complaining secretary and interrupted a meeting with two planners, serious young men in shirtsleeves armed with large maps of the town. In the face of Mickey's intrusion, Mayor Jock Whitlock remained surprisingly calm.

"I need to talk to you," Mickey said.

"This is not the way to do it," Jock said.

"It is when it involves your niece," Mickey replied.

Jock nodded at the two planners and said, "Our meeting is adjourned, gentlemen."

The two young men collected their maps and made a hasty exit. Jock sat behind his massive desk and said, "Okay, Mickey. What's this all about?"

"You own a cabin in Caledon. Tell me where I can find it."

Whatever Jock might have been expecting Mickey to demand, that certainly wasn't it. He spoke slowly: "Supposing I was to say something like, I don't know what you're talking about."

"Look, Jean has gone up there alone. A man is after her, and he may have followed her."

Jock swallowed and said, "She's there now?"

"I think so, yeah. And maybe in a lot of trouble. So, please, Jock, let's forgo the usual bullshit. Tell me how to get to the cabin."

"About forty minutes northeast of here, near Bel-fountain," Jock said.

"Give me the address," Mickey said.

52

She must have dozed off. One moment she was awake, the next her head was jerking up, drawing her out of a deep sleep. She swore to herself for being so careless. The thunder seemed to have subsided, but the rain continued to fall, beating against the roof.

Feeling stiff, beginning to regret her choice of chair, Jean stood, stretching, coming into full wakefulness. That was better she thought, thinking she would drink more water and perhaps have another granola bar. That would revive her.

She bent to her carryall on the floor just as something flashed in the air around her; she glimpsed a curved knife blade. Somehow—perhaps hesitating an instant too long—it missed her throat, slicing instead into her shoulder. Searing pain, the spreading warmth of blood. She ducked back as the blade swept in again, this time cutting into her torso. She twisted around, falling against the end table. Blindly, she grabbed at the baton.

Something—someone!—jolted against her. Instinctively she extended the baton, lashing out. That produced a grunt of pain, enough for the moment she needed to shoot forward to the door. She managed to get it open and then throw herself into the rainy night.

Racing full out, Jean managed a glance behind her, caught a glimpse of her pursuer bursting out the doorway after her. She pushed herself harder as she clambered up the hill, tripped over something, stumbling, fighting to keep her balance.

———————

The rain let up a bit as Mickey turned onto Wellington Road. His windshield wipers—he had meant to get the goddamn things changed—served only to obscure his view of the thin strip of roadway in front of him. He swore, pounding at the wheel, loudly lamenting how shit always happened just when you needed shit not to happen.

He clamped on the gas and his car lurched forward, fishtailing across the wet pavement. For a second, he thought he would lose control, but the car righted itself. Not nearly fast enough, though. The goddamn clunker he should have gotten rid of long ago.

Through the smeared windshield, the road lay straight and rain-swept.

53

In the darkness and rain, Jean stopped suddenly and spun around.

Lashing out with the baton. Smashing it against the side of her pursuer's head. That failed to stop him. She swung again, missed, and that provided the opening needed to slam her to the muddy ground. The air burst out of her. Vaguely, she was aware of a dark figure. She had the presence of mind to slam the baton between his legs. That provoked a cry of pain.

He reeled back, suddenly caught in headlights. Jean glimpsed the shiny grill of a metallic beast charging headlong. There was a loud *wumph*! Her pursuer was launched into the air. The metallic beast slowed, as if to measure the distance to the spot where the intruder had landed and lay groaning and writhing in the mud.

Then the beast shot forward rolling over the fallen intruder. A scream and the metallic beast shot past the crumpled body. In the crimson glow of its taillights, Jean, rose to her feet to view the anguished, shattered face of Shaar Zorn.

She now saw that the big metal killing machine was a Ford truck. It had come to a stop. The driver's-side door opened and Adam Machota hopped to the ground.

The man who had come to town to kill her had killed the man who was supposed to save her.

Then it struck her: it might not have been Shaar Zorn Machota had intended to run down.

It might have been her.

She turned and started running again. Behind her, she could hear Machota's voice through the rain: "Jean!"

She kept going, realizing she no longer had the baton, nothing with which to fight. Her only hope was to outrun Machota.

He yelled her name a second time; she sensed him gaining on her. The rain came down harder than before, silvery sleet-like lines cutting through the blackness.

Then something—some sort of weird survival instinct, perhaps—made her pull up. Not a moment too soon, for now she found herself staring into the abyss or—more accurately—the blackness beyond the edge of the rift.

Machota drew near.

She pivoted, throwing herself at him, clawing at his face. For a moment, Machota was thrown off guard by the ferociousness of her attack. They wrestled together, the wind blowing the rain against them.

As she struggled, Machota wrapped his arms around her, drawing her close. His lips touched at her ear. She heard him breathe a single word: "Together..."

And then they were locked in each other's embrace, tumbling into the blackness. She had an instant to ponder the incongruity of this, that she would die with the man she hated; he had killed her as she had killed him.

The rift reached up and pulled them down to earth, Machota crashing against the rocks with Jean on top of him.

She rolled off him, everything hurting. There was a bright flash of lightning and a violent crack of thunder. In that brief blaze of light, she saw him, splayed like a rag doll, not moving. Then the returning darkness swallowed him. She lay there, gazing up at the pelting rain coming down on her. She would lie there forever. There was nothing left.

Then she heard him.

She managed to turn her head. The rag doll stirred beside her. In the darkness she could see his lips move.

"…there early…" he muttered.

"What?"

His mouth moved again, but this time she couldn't make out what he said. "What is it, Adam?"

"Here…" he mumbled.

She managed to shift her body around on the rocks. Fierce knives of pain stabbed through her. She lifted her head a bit so that her ear was close to his lips.

"What, Adam? What are you trying to say?"

"Saw it…"

"Saw what?"

"Desiree…"

"You were there," Jean said. "You killed her."

His lips moved forming a word: "No…"

Silence. Jean strained closer to him. "Then who, Adam? Who killed her?"

His mouth opened and closed, as if he was trying to form words, unable to muster the strength.

"Who, Adam?"

A light shaft from above caused her to squint. An angel arriving to take her to that better place she had heard so much about as a child.

Machota's mouth opened again and this time a single word emerged clearly: "Ryan."

Adam Machota stopped moving.

Jean sank against the rocks. Her pain was overwhelming. The light from above caressed her.

The angel called, "Jean? Are you all right?"

That didn't sound like any angel she could imagine. The voice called again: "Jean, answer me. Are you all right?"

Mickey Dann.

Not an angel, exactly. But close enough.

54

Jean had spent hours being debriefed by Inspector Gordon Castle of the Royal Canadian Mounted Police. She liked him. Unlike others in the Mountie hierarchy with whom she had been forced to deal, he came across as an honest, reliable guy.

"Jill Lowry and Adam Machota wanted you gone from the Force because of what they were afraid you knew about their criminal activities," Castle explained during one of their sessions together.

"But I didn't know anything," Jean protested.

"They weren't about to take that chance," Castle said. "Then things got complicated when Lowry realized Machota had become obsessed with you. That's when she came to Milton. That's what got her killed."

It was Castle who now urged her to come back to the Force. "It's going to take a lot of hard work for us to regain public trust after what's happened," he said. "We're going to need people like you to help make that happen."

"I'd be surprised if they would want me back."

"This has already been discussed at the highest levels," Castle said. "I've been authorized to say that you would be welcomed with open arms."

But Jean wasn't sure she wanted to go back. The Force had been her life; all she had ever wanted was to be a Mountie. But now that she was no longer part of it, she had come to the realization that, at this point in her life, she might want something else.

The question was, what? What did she want?

She didn't have the answer.

Well, that wasn't quite true. She had *part* of the answer. A very important part.

This time Jean phoned Grace to arrange the meeting. "He'll be delighted," Grace said.

"So, you're still with him," Jean said.

"I wouldn't know where else to go," Grace said, sounding resigned. "Your uncle is what he is, and I guess I am what I am, and more the fool for it, but what can you do?"

"As long as he doesn't bring sandwiches," Jean said. "I don't want anything from him, least of all a sandwich."

"It's not the sandwiches he's interested in," Grace said.

"No?"

"I believe he's looking for forgiveness."

"Let's see about that," Jean said.

"Don't hurt him." Grace's voice took on a firmness Jean had not heard before.

"The usual place," Jean said. "Tell him the usual place. Make sure he's there."

———

Jock brought sandwiches, anyway. "Ham and cheese," he said once she had joined him on the bench.

"If you're tired of tuna, I thought you might like ham and cheese."

Rather than argue, Jean sighed and accepted the proffered sandwich.

"Your arm's still in a sling, I see," Jock said, after biting into his sandwich. "How are you doing otherwise?"

"Aching in a lot of places I never ached in before," Jean said. "But I'm okay."

"You stirred up a shitstorm," Jock said. "Exposing a mini-drug cartel operating inside the RCMP overseen by Inspector Jill Lowry, linked to the Afghan police and Major Shaar Zorn with Adam Machota acting as liaison. Have I got all that right?"

"Pretty much," Jean said.

"What about this guy Zorn? I'm having trouble figuring him. I thought he was supposed to protect you."

"I thought so, too. He had saved my life in Kandahar, probably because he thought he could use me against Machota."

"Which he did."

"What no one realized, least of all Machota and Jill Lowry, was that Shaar was actually working in his country's best interests. He set out to destroy the drug network he supposedly was part of, and that meant killing anyone who got in his way, including Machota and me."

"But you exposed those bastards, Jean. You risked your life to do it. You're a hero."

"I didn't set out to expose anything, just survive a crazy man who burned down my house, got Mickey framed, his career nearly ruined, and me almost killed."

"And murdered my Desiree," Jock said.

"No, he didn't do that," Jean said.

Jock made a face. "What are you talking about?"

"You did it, Jock. You and Tara Ryan. You murdered Desiree."

Jock went silent. He looked away, as though digesting what he had just heard, gathering his thoughts, mustering his arguments. "Are you wearing a wire, Jean?"

"Why? Are you about to make a confession?"

"I told you a hundred times, I didn't do it." He placed his uneaten sandwich on the bench, as though a barrier between them, protecting him from her accusations.

"What I couldn't understand at first is why you would want me involved in your scheme," Jean said.

"Scheme? There was no scheme." Jock sounded indignant.

"But then you probably figured if you had a former Mountie working for you, it would make a blackmail plan all the more plausible. What you didn't figure was Desiree bringing me along. Not that it mattered. I got there too late to help her."

"Jean, I have no idea what you're talking about."

"You almost pulled it off, Jock. Your wife, blackmailed by a mysterious lover, shows up to make a payoff and is murdered. At that time of day in a remote mall in Acton, there would be no witnesses."

"Jean stop this." Jock sounded angry.

"Except there was a witness."

"Yeah? Who was this witness?"

"Adam Machota."

Jock looked less angry, more amazed. "Adam Machota is dead. You killed him."

"Before he died, he told me that he witnessed her murder."

"This is bullshit," Jock said. But he wasn't looking at her when he said it.

"The police have found Tara in Winnipeg. She's confessed to her part in the murder. They're flying her back here now."

Jock turned to her, his face the color of chalk. "I'm your uncle for Christ's sake."

"Which is why I had such a hard time getting my head around all this. You sent Tara to talk to me, hoping that by admitting she was sleeping with you and Desiree it would throw me off. And it almost worked. I thought you were careless and self-centered and deceitful, but I didn't think you could kill your wife. But it was the last thing Machota told me; his final gift of pain. If he wanted to devastate me, he certainly succeeded."

A car pulled up to the curb and came to a stop. Mickey Dann got out, followed by detectives Glen Petrusiak and Indira Kobus.

Stricken, Jock said, "God, Jean, what have you done?"

Jean stared at her uneaten sandwich. She stood up. "You know what, Jock? I don't think I'm a ham and cheese person."

Indira Kobus came to a stop in front of Jock, her face set in a grim expression. Jock looked up at her with dull eyes. She said, "Mayor, I'm Detective Indira Kobus. I'd like you to come with me."

"What's this about?"

"I have some questions that pertain to the murder of your wife. We need you to come to police headquarters."

Jock didn't move. "I need to phone my lawyer."

"You can do that when we get to police headquarters," Detective Kobus said.

Petrusiak stepped forward and said, "Would you stand up, please, mayor?"

Jock looked alarmed. "You're not going to handcuff me, are you?"

"No, sir," Petrusiak answered. "But we need you to come with us now."

Jock struggled to his feet. The three detectives stepped back, as though he might make a run for it.

Jock gave Jean a withering look, and said, "Take care of yourself, Jean."

He walked away unsteadily. Petrusiak and Indira Kobus trailed after him.

She watched the detectives open the rear door of their car. Jock ducked inside. Indira got in beside him.

Jean adjusted her arm in the sling again and saw Mickey Dann walking back to her. "I wanted to make sure you're okay," he said.

"I just turned in my uncle, the guy I grew up envying and admiring," she said.

"He might have avoided any of this by not killing his wife," he said.

Jean didn't say anything.

Mickey broke the awkward silence by asking, "How's the arm?"

"Broken," Jean answered.

Mickey shrugged. "Stupid question, I guess."

"I wasn't expecting you to show up today," Jean said.

"I've been reinstated in the department. All sorts of shit going down over Machota and his gang of redcoats. Now this. Turns out they may need me after all."

"Glad you're back," Jean said. "Milton's a much safer place with you around. How are you doing, anyway?"

"Getting through, I guess. Trying to shake off a couple of hundred thousand regrets."

"Reagan?"

"She crosses my mind every so often, yeah."

"I'm sorry," she said.

He brightened. "Hey, I heard you may become a Mountie again."

"I don't know," Jean said. "I haven't made up my mind."

"I keep thinking about that time."

"What time was that?"

"The time when, for want of a better word, you seduced me."

"I never seduced you. I *distracted* you."

"There's not much of a difference."

"There's a big difference."

"Well, something sure as hell happened."

"Yes," she said. "Something sure as hell did."

"The question is, what?"

"You can't figure that out?"

"Nope, I can't."

She started across the street. He called out, "That's it?"

She turned, smiling. "Call me sometime, maybe we can figure it out together."

Jean continued on. Mickey watched her.

Shaking his head.

Acknowledgments

The team that supports my novels worked overtime to get *The Mill Pond* into shape. David Kendall, whose input has become invaluable, arrived back in Canada after an eighteen-hour flight from Australia and almost immediately went to work saving my derriere.

Ray Bennett, best pal and superb writer and editor, in the midst of moving flats in London, England, somehow found the time to edit the book.

Rebecca Hunter, Milton reader extraordinaire, interrupted her busy life as director of the J. Scott Early Funeral Home to read through the manuscript. The fact that I burned down her house—only in the book, mind you—didn't faze her at all.

Whenever I'm having trouble creating a strong, intelligent, independent woman in my novels, I have only to think of my wife, Kathy, and the writing suddenly becomes much easier. Not only does she inspire me daily in our life together, but she is also first reader—and critic—and, as with everything else she brings to our marriage, I am so much better for it.

And, of course, I couldn't do any of this without the support of my brother, Ric, partner and co-conspirator when it comes to the operation of West-End Books and the novels it publishes.

Jennifer Smith once again brought her creative brilliance to *The Mill Pond's* cover.

Finally, I have to thank the people of Milton, Ontario, the town west of Toronto that has not only embraced Kathy and me, but puts up with an author who, among other shortcomings, leaves dead bodies at the Mill Pond.

––––––––––

Readers should know there is a real place called Milton. From Toronto, you drive west an hour or so (depending on traffic), turn south on Highway 25, and soon you have reached the town. That's the real Milton. The Milton you have read about in the previous pages, while accurate insofar as setting, is, nonetheless, a fictional Milton, the Milton out of this author's slightly diabolical imagination.

www.ronbase.com
Read Ron's blog at
www.ronbase.wordpress.com
Contact Ron at
ronbase@ronbase.com

If You Enjoyed *The Mill Pond*, don't miss

Ron Base's

THE ESCARPMENT

Disgraced Royal Canadian Mounted Police officer Jean Whitlock returns home to Milton, the town west of Toronto where she grew up. She is staying with her younger brother, Bryce, who runs the family funeral business. An early morning phone call brings them up to the escarpment to pick up the body of a young woman.

Jean, haunted by her own demons, finds herself drawn into the mystery of the woman's death. She unearths long-buried secrets, not only in her own life, but the town's as well. Powerful local forces are working against her. Jean's life is in danger. In a town full of shadows and lies, nothing is as it seems.